About the Editor

Violet Barungi was born in Mbarara district, Western Uganda and has a BA in History from Makerere University Kampala. She has published two novels, *Cassandra* and *The Shadow and The Substance,* and a collection of short stories for childrenm, *Tit for Tat and other stories.* Her play, *Over My Dead Body,* won the British Council International New Playwriting Award for Africa and the Middle East 1997. Her short story, *Kefa Kazana*, in *Origin East Africa*, an anthology of short stories edited by Prof. David Cook, was broadcast on BBC. Violet Barungi also edited the first anthology of short stories by Ugandan women writers. She works as an editor for FEMRITE.

i

WORDS FROM A GRANARY

An anthology of short stories
BY Ugandan Women Writers
Edited by
Violet Barungi

FEMRITE Publications Limited
Kampala

FEMRITE Publications Limited
P. O. Box 705, Tel. 543943
KAMPALA, Uganda

Printed in Uganda by **The New Vision**.

ISBN-9970 700 01 4

INTRODUCTION

Words From a Granary is the long-awaited sequel to *A Woman's Voice*. As we brainstormed on the title to give our second anthology of short stories, we came up with the word, *granary*. In traditional Africa, no homestead is ever without a granary, and no granary is ever empty. A granary is a symbol of hope where there would be despair; it is a symbol of promise in what would be a hopeless situation. Likewise, Ugandan women writers refuse to be discouraged by the appalling lack of a reading culture in the country. They keep wielding their pens, churning out more and more reading material in the hope that one day, our people will realise that reading is the backbone of intellectual empowerment and an integral part of development.

In our call for short stories to be published in an anthology, emphasis was put on originality, creativity and readability. No thematic restrictions were set, leaving the choice of topics to the authors. The results were not disappointing: more than 30 short stories were received, out of which 15 were selected.

The anthology is the outcome of a three-year programme of training workshops geared towards equipping creative women writers with writing skills. It was made possible through the financial support of our funders, HIVOS, who sponsored the training workshops as well as the publication of the book.

Many thanks go to the writers, too, for their commitment to the promotion of the reading culture in the country by contributing to the scanty reading material.

Lastly, I want to acknowledge the great effort put in by members of the FEMRITE Editorial Board to bring the stories to the required standard. These are:

Mary Karooro Okurut
Hilda Twongyeirwe Rutagonya
Ayeta Anne Wangusa
Winnie Munyarugerero

Violet Barungi
Editor.

CONTENTS

I Watch You My Sister

Goretti Kyomuhendo

I watch you, my sister, sitting in the same spot you have always sat for the last ten years. Even as we went through the throes of a terrible war in this country, you never abandoned your place. Even as everything was razed to the ground, everything looted from the stores, everything except books; you never deserted your favourite spot.

Even when everyone ran in disarray; even as the bullets flew above your head, you still sat head held high, unmoving, in your abode. Even as the fair-skinned tall men dressed in camouflaged fatigues roamed the city at night, arresting anyone breaking the curfew, you still sat in the same spot.

I watch you, my sister, clutching your little treasures around you: an empty, dirty, rusty, 'Kimbo' tin — your safe; two wooden legs safely tucked away under your tattered blankets and your two little ones, their faces a mask of bewildered empty stares, their shoulders haggard.

I watch you, my sister, stretching your thin arms to receive your hastily proffered gifts whilst murmuring a prayer to your deaf God. I listen to you as you sing your well-rehearsed anthem, with your little ones chorusing along. The only change I see is in your surroundings. Just near your throne, stands the newly refurbished, imposing Grand Imperial Hotel, the Speke Hotel and The Sheraton Hotel. I watch you as you let your misty eyes feast on the sparkling, multicoloured, dancing neon lights emanating from these grand structures. What a hefty meal for your eyes!

I watch you as you stare and salivate at the bigger neon lights that announce great and delicious world cuisine: Chinese Food, Indian Curry, Italian Ice Cream, and American Pizza. I wonder why they never announce the African delicacies?

I watch you as your next bait approaches. A policeman, eeeh…a traffic policeman! He looks tired, my sister, and I wonder if he will hear your memorised song or see your outstretched hand.

"*Baba, Baba, mpayo akokulya* (give me something small to eat)", you still intone, anyway.

Without turning to look at you, he dips his tired hand in his pocket and brings out crumpled, hastily folded notes. But he puts them back and comes out with a more suitable gift for you: a shining two hundred-shilling coin, which he carelessly throws in your open safe. Alas, it misses the safe and falls right in the latrine of the little ones.

I see them scurrying excitedly to retrieve the family's lost treasure. The little one does not see the taxdriver, who is driving insanely and hooting madly trying to attract his own baits. He runs straight into her.

How you scream, my sister, how you cry, how you weep! How you implore your deaf God! How I wish both your legs were not wooden stumps tucked away in your blankets!

I watch you, my sister, once again with your little treasures around you, only this time, there is only one little one.

Aaah, here comes another bait. What bait! What a mountain of a woman! She parks her mammoth of a car, which occupies two parking spaces and one tyre comes to sit on your wooden legs.

"Mama, Mama, mpayo akokulya..."

The huge lady is wiggling her fat behind out of the car, clutching her leather handbag more tightly. She is now walking towards you and I can see lots of smiles hidden behind your tears. She is swinging her buttocks carelessly, clicking her high heels on the tarmac pavement noisily. The strong January wind blows her slit-skirt this way and that way, revealing pink knickers. She stops to remove her shades, then dips a meticulously manicured hand, with fingers littered with gold rings, into her leather handbag and comes out with a blue handkerchief.

"Mama...Mama..."

"Oh these beggars!" She screws up her nose and quickly scurries past you. She is late for a meeting, my sister. She has to attend that important meeting the huge banner is announcing at the Sheraton Hotel: 'Laying Strategies For the Plan of Action and Celebrating the Achievements of the Fair Gender in the New Millennium'.

I watch you, my sister, as your final bait for the day approaches. Eeeh, a white man, this time. Once again, your eyes are full of those bottomless smiles, your song louder...

"Muzungu, Muzungu,mpayo akokulya..."

The *Muzungu* smiles at you, that plastic, crack-of-a face smile. He tightens his hold on the papers under his arm and almost breaks into a run. But the little one is on his heels, tugging at his white trousers and this time, he actually runs, and keeps on running until he is in the safety of the Grand Imperial Hotel.

What a world, my sister! I wonder what keeps you going. What keeps you so alert, my sister? I need not ask, for the answer is in your eyes: the smells. The strange floating smells from the world's cuisine, mixed with the stench from the little one's latrine, mingling with the strong smells of the contents of the disposed rubbers strewn carelessly near your home by impatient night lovers...

Floating Images

Sandra Aimo Okoed

The professor's authoritative voice boomed through the lecture theatre. Sylvia stole into the room and scanned the front row for her favourite seat. A sea of cold indifferent stares met her intense gaze. She rubbed her eyes and squinted as she tried to make out the images before her.

"Can you please find a seat: you are disrupting my lecture," the professor shouted.

She felt a flush of heat spread through the back of her neck. She clutched her clipboard to her chest and made her way up the blurred stairs. Left foot right foot, left foot...she was getting tired of concentrating on the stairs. God forbid if she missed a step and fell...

There it was...an empty place. "Move over," Sylvia said in her most authoritative voice. The young man begrudgingly scooted over, causing the entire row to move in a ripple-like fashion.

She settled into the uncomfortably warm seat, opened up her clipboard and grabbed a pen. Her heart sank as she looked at the blackboard. It just could not be real! All she could make out were blurred images on the board. She shut her eyes, opened them: the situation remained the same...shapeless white symbols continued to float about on the black-board.

At closer range, the situation was better. The letters in the notebook sprang up as if to greet her. Back to the blackboard, the symbols continued to do their thing...float, float, float. They refused to remain still.

As the anxiety intensified within, her mouth went painfully dry. Then, as if that were not enough, tiny beads of sweat erupted all over her body, positioning themselves on her forehead, nose, neck, and back. This was getting serious. She had always known that she had a problem with her sight but had managed to get by. She recalled the taunts and abuse that her mates had dished out during break. "Goody, goody," their voices were so fresh in her mind that her eyes began to smart. If only she had the guts to tell them that she had to sit in the front to see the blackboard.

The professor's voice brought her back to the lecture hall. Sylvia enviously looked over at her neighbour who was studiously scribbling away. He was getting knowledge, information that she too needed to pass her exams. How would she explain failing her exams to her parents! Her father was a self-made businessman who took pride in his modest beginnings, while her mother was a headmistress of a secondary school.

She discreetly placed her right hand on the desk and slowly moved her middle finger to the corner of her left eye and raised it. That did the trick…she had learnt it while in secondary school, compliments of a short -sighted friend. The letters on the board slowly arranged themselves to form words she could recognise. The more of the sentence she read, the bigger the smile that formed on her face. All of a sudden, the professor raised the duster and sealed her fate: he erased the writing on the board. Sylvia's eyes stung as the reality of the action dawned on her. Feelings of anger, frustration and pain tore at each other. She shifted her body from side to side, hoping to create a passage for the cauldron of emotions to seep through. Determined not to let this state of mind affect her, she sat upright, placed her finger on the side of her left eye, pulled at it and started taking down notes.

With each stroke of the professor's chalk, the more her throat burned and eyes smarted. What if he, in his fit of intellect, again erased the precious kernels from the board? The frenzied writing on the board stopped as the professor placed a full stop at the end of the sentence.

"Complete this assignment for next week," was all she heard. The rustling of papers and shuffling of feet signalled the end of the lecture.

"Can you move?" said an irritated bass. She had blocked part of the row.

"What are you doing, we have to catch other lectures," said another.

Sylvia scooted out of the way. The students' laughter and murmurs stung her like salt on a wound. They can talk because they don't have to suffer, she thought to herself.

Sylvia picked up her clipboard and moved towards the front of the hall to the place that she selfishly called hers. At her place, the writing on the board stood out like a freshly painted zebra crossing. Eager to understand what she did not really comprehend, she moved over to the second row. Here, the words on the blackboard began to swim but she could still make out a few of them. Third row, the words started to cause havoc…not only were they swimming but they were blurred beyond recognition! The severity of the problem hit her like a ton of bricks; she needed glasses, a life altering change…

Florence would definitely laugh at her, while Jenny and Harriet would sympathise. Who is she deceiving, they would laugh at her behind her back. Sylvia tore her mind off the scenario that she had so carefully played out. Then his image slowly crept into her mind...what about him? Her palms began to sweat as she quickly closed her notebook ...are you kidding, Sylvia? Don't run away from the truth. He is going to chuck you in a second. Who wants a four-eyed girlfriend? How would he kiss you with your glasses on? What if they got too foggy while you are kissing? Remember Deborah who went to a dance? They say that she intimidated the boys all because she wore glasses. What about the nasty names that boys call girls who wear glasses... 'four eyes,' 'ugly,'...no! 'Book-worm,' 'wise-ass'... not me!

***

"What are you doing at home?" her brother asked.

"It's good to see you as well," she replied. "So what's new?"

"Oh nothing - the *zeyis* are the same. I think the old man is going senile, though. Yesterday he was talking about the house he is going to build for grand-ma, which we all know was completed a year ago - unless we have another grandmother we don't know about," he chuckled.

As brother and sister were busy catching up on each other's lives, Sylvia's mother entered the room. "Sylvia, you are home! Welcome!"

Sylvia turned around and moved towards her mother. She stuck out her hand only to be pulled into a bone-breaking hug. "Mommy, I can't breathe!" she cried. She loved her mother dearly but now that she was no longer a child, the two just did not feel right.

An hour into the conversation, Sylvia mustered enough courage to break the news, "Mommy, I came to see you because I need glasses," she said.

"How long have you known this?" her mother asked.

"A little while now."

"And you didn't tell us?" she remarked.

"I thought I could handle it," Sylvia said in a whisper.

"What do you mean handle it," asked her mother. "Spoilt eyesight will not just fix itself!" Her voice took on an unmistakably caustic tone. "I will talk it over with your father when he comes home. When are you planning to go back to school?" she added.

"Tomorrow." Sylvia slowly got off the sofa, left the house and settled under the jacaranda tree. "Oh jacaranda tree, why me?" she asked loudly as she rested her head against the mossy trunk. She closed her eyes and drifted off to sleep.

"Sylvia, wake up," her brother said as he tapped her shoulder. "Daddy's

6

home."

She ambled onto her feet and headed for the house. As she entered, her brother tenderly squeezed her elbow. "It will be all right," he said as he left her.

Her parents were seated in the living room. Her father looked glum, the day's activities written all over his face, while her mother's face had a maternal smile plastered over it.

"It's good to see you and see that you are well," her father said, as he motioned her to sit. "Now, your mother tells me that you need glasses. Is that true?" he asked.

"Yes, it is," Sylvia responded.

"When did you discover that you had this problem?"

"It has been a problem since secondary school, but it has just got worse," she said.

"It's definitely a first in our family," he said flatly as he adjusted his necktie. "What exactly is the problem?"

"I cannot see the blackboard during lectures."

"So it means that you are near-sighted," he interjected.

"It seems."

"OK, you should make an appointment with an optician for this weekend. Your mother and I will work out the finances," he said, rubbing his hands.

***

"Sit here and look at the wall," Dr. Deepak said as he motioned to a solitary stool in the middle of the spotlessly white room. "Tell me which is clearer," he said. Sylvia was wearing a crude set of glasses with thick frames and lenses. The clinking of the discs falling on top of each other caused her ears to ring. As some of the letters on the wall got clearer, others got more blurred. Clink, clink, clink…This did not stop Dr. Deepak. He kept on adding and removing lenses as if he were playing with a toy. "It appears that your left eye is weaker than your right," he said in a self-important manner. "Hmmm," he grunted. His *hmmm* broke the cold silence in the room. "Can you see the letters on the wall?" he asked.

Sylvia self-consciously nodded her head in an effort to keep the contraption on the bridge of her pudgy nose.

"Please read them out loud." Sylvia did. "Perfect," he said, scratching his coffee brown clean-shaven chin. He quickly scribbled something on a piece of paper and handed it to her. "Please see the lady at the counter," he said showing her out of the room.

As Sylvia settled the bill, the young woman behind the counter informed her that she would have to choose the frame. The pair of glasses, she added in a matter of-fact-manner, would be ready that afternoon.

Frames were an accessory that either made or broke your appearance, thought Sylvia. After what seemed hours of trying on several styles, Sylvia spotted a pair of small black frames with gold speckles. The lady, who had not left her side since the process begun now slowly unlocked the case and handed the pair of glasses to Sylvia. Sylvia stood in front of the mirror, hesitated, then slowly raised the frame to her face to finally put it on. Hmmm...not too bad, she thought. "Yes, I think I like this," she said.

Sylvia and the silent woman went to the counter where yet another woman told her to collect her pair of glasses in the afternoon.

"Here are your glasses, miss," said an Asian woman behind the counter in the afternoon. She handed Sylvia the pair of glasses. "What kind of case would you like, hard or soft?"

"A hard one," Sylvia replied.

"Why don't you try on your glasses?" the woman asked as she pointed over to a mirror above the counter.

Sylvia timidly got the glasses out of the case and slowly placed the contraption on her face. The Asian woman nodded her head as she scrutinised Sylvia's glasses. "You made a good choice of frame," she said after a long silence.

Sylvia slowly raised her head to meet the *new her*. The reflection in the mirror stared back at her. She turned to the left, then to the right, staring at herself in the mirror. As she studied her new image, she noticed that her frames emphasised her high cheekbones and gave her a sort of a sophisticated look.

They are not bad, not bad, not bad, Sylvia thought nodding her head. As she stepped out onto the sidewalk, the world looked no longer the cold and hostile place it had been a few days ago. The cars, the people, the buildings, they were all within reach now. The street signs and shop names were legible, but with this new lease on life came the ugliness, the cracks in the pavement, the dirt, the grime, the poverty of the city...

As she walked down the street, she passed a pack of boys idly chatting away. As the group made its way along the busy street, one of the boys trailed behind and quickly closed and opened his left eye - he had winked at her! The boy had actually winked at her! There was no question about it; she was going to wear the glasses!

Rogue Male

Josephine Wanja

Where Caleb was born, I never knew. That is to say, the exact village of his birth. I, of course, knew roughly where he came from and he came with references to some earlier jobs he had done. I wondered later whether his erstwhile employers had given him references only to assure themselves that he would never bother them again. But then Caleb was plausible, friendly, and often useful. So maybe he had not stayed with any long enough to show his true colours.

I employed Caleb as a cook and general factotum. His cooking was rudimentary, but then I was not at a stage in my life when gourmet meals were likely to be required. I was, to begin with, itinerant, with no fixed abode. I was carrying out a comparative anthropological study. In case this will immediately put off the less academic reader, let me explain that what I was actually doing was comparing how small farmers in different places responded to the advice given them by agricultural officers on how to cultivate a variety of crops.

The study involved a lot of travelling between places where I was studying the different groups of farmers. What I needed was someone who would prepare a basic meal, wash my clothes and clean whatever house I was staying in at any one time. And who did not mind being on the move.

Caleb liked travelling, going to different places, meeting different people, and as it turned out, meeting lots of different ladies. He was even helpful to me in my researches as, through various contacts, he often got a slant on things that eluded me. The farmers and their wives and daughters took to him as one of themselves and often told him thoughts and doings that they wished to conceal from me.

We travelled in a Peugeot car, of what is now ancient vintage, but then a contemporary model. We took most of what we needed, including camp beds, cooking stoves and pots, as well as our clothes and other personal necessities.

I paid Caleb a regular salary, average for those times, and was fairly

9

liberal in providing other side benefits. I did not object when he pilfered my cigarettes. I loaned him money to buy a bicycle that took ages to pay back. I photographed him in arrogant poses next to the bicycle to show off to all his relatives back wherever he came from. He ate what I ate and usually there was nothing left of the stew, or whatever, that we had each day. As we did not have a refrigerator most of the time, this was probably as well.

I also did not object, as some employers do, to his stream of visitors. There was always a group, seated around in his room. I also never questioned the cost of anything he purchased from the market, though I knew he probably added a bit as profit for himself. For Caleb was at heart an entrepreneur. He never missed an opportunity for making something on the side.

He was also, as I have said, something of a ladies' man. Women liked him. Women loved him, especially bored wives of farmers whose husbands lacked finesse. Young girls too, who were equally bored with the boys they had gone to school with and already knew too well. This stranger, not only was exotic, but also was actually good looking and had a regular income. The farmers had irregular incomes from selling crops, or the occasional chicken or goat, mostly to cover major expenses. And the boys often had nothing, depending on their fathers for handouts, or from casual work like digging for someone else.

Among them, Caleb was a prince. He knew how to talk his way into a girl's heart, into a woman's affections, and more to the point, into her bed, or rather, his. And this gave rise to the first of the problems I had with Caleb.

The camp beds we had had been issued with by the Research Institute for which I worked, were the normal type of camp bed. Rather flimsy in structure, not heavy duty wooden ones. And Caleb's style of lovemaking, although I had no personal experience of it, must have been very active, to say the least. Athletic, manly, and definitely not brief and unsatisfactory for the women.

The result was that the beds did not stand up to the strain. Bed after bed crumpled, legs bent, canvas sagging. They had to be returned to the Institute, which could not understand what on earth I was doing with them that their life expectancy should be so short. Bed after bed had to be replaced until I received a severe warning from the director. After that, I told Caleb to use the floor until he was ready to sleep, and that if the lady was weighty, the floor was the best place to sleep.

The ladies he courted were, to my observation, catholic to an extreme. Not religiously Catholic, or if they were, they must have spent much time at their Confessions, but catholic in the sense of being of a wide variety of ethnic backgrounds, shapes, sizes, educational levels and social standing. In fact, Caleb could have carried out a most useful supplementary research on the women of these areas we were working in. I, of course dealt mainly with men, as most of the farmers were men. Women who owned farms were at that time very few in number.

Caleb was, as I said, welcome to my cigarettes and was, incidentally, a major factor in my eventually giving up smoking, since as soon as I opened a packet and smoked one, the rest seemed to evaporate, and literally go up in smoke. It got so expensive, and whenever I wanted one, the packet was empty and the shop far away, that I dropped the habit.

What Caleb did not make me give up, however, was drinking coffee. One may wonder what was the connection between coffee and cigarettes, although both are said to be equally bad for one's health, if coffee is slightly less so than cigarettes. The problem, however, was not health related, but arose out of Caleb's flair for business.

I used to buy those extra large tins of instant coffee. But although it was only myself and Caleb drinking it, plus the occasional visitor, somehow, one tin only lasted for about two weeks. Sugar also disappeared at a phenomenal rate, but then I knew that although I was abstemious myself, taking at most one teaspoon in a large cup, other people could put in two or even three dessertspoonfuls. One wondered if they were drinking coffee (or tea for that matter) or sugared flavoured milk. Milk was also added in quantity to the cup or for tea cooked Indian fashion by boiling it together with milk, water and spices, milk being a bigger proportion of the brew than water.

But my consumption of coffee puzzled me. Whenever questioned, Caleb was evasive or stated blandly that I must be drinking more than I thought. Then one day, I arrived home unexpectedly in the middle of the morning and found him reclining at ease on a sofa, while a strange man was industriously cleaning the room. My perplexity was evident, and eventual annoyance, not to say anger patent, but Caleb was unrepentant. He did not even have the grace to be apologetic. The man was helping him. He was helping him in return for liberal cups of coffee. That was why my coffee was disappearing at such a great rate. Caleb did not work. He paid others to do it all, at my expense, with my coffee and sugar. I was perhaps surprised that the labourers were happy to accept so small a payment for their endeavours.

Caleb had proved useful in other respects, so after a warning and the precaution of locking up my coffee tin, he continued working for me while looking for other opportunities to exercise his undoubted talents for making money with the least effort and outlay. One of these schemes involved me in an abortive business venture, on my side. My business ventures, unlike those of Caleb, had invariably been expensive and unprofitable, it must be said. This one probably made money for Caleb but certainly, not for me.

It involved shipping agricultural produce by rail to a town in a neighbouring country. In one of the places we stayed in, there was both a railway station and a plentiful supply of agricultural products. The produce was destined for a large commercial centre where there was a high demand for bananas and other foodstuff.

For some weeks, I gave Caleb money to buy bananas, and they were routinely loaded onto the train and taken off the other end by Caleb's cousin for sale. Since the cousin did not have to pay anything for them, he definitely made a profit. Unfortunately, the system for shipping the money back in return for the bananas proved rather less efficient than the railway for carrying goods. So after some time, and increasing drains on my purse, this enterprise was abandoned.

Caleb's enthusiasm for commerce was, however, unabated. He continued to use every opportunity for exercising his talents for business. Some I probably never got to know about which was just as well, but at least two involved me personally. In both cases, I never knew how long the illicit activities had been going on. But probably not an extensive period of time, since they were carried out in a house I eventually settled in and stayed for about a year.

One day, as in the earlier case, I returned home unexpectedly. Caleb was not present. However, someone else was. Going into the bathroom, I found a strange man washing his clothes in my English style bath, with my soap powder and my hot water. He was vigorously scrubbing away at several mundane garments, trousers, shirts and underpants. They were most certainly not my clothes. So Caleb was not up to his old tricks of getting someone else to do his work.

The guy was not at all bothered by my sudden appearance. He told me, "It's okay, I've paid Caleb." After further consultation, I discovered that Caleb had been renting out my facilities for a small fee to his friends, and their friends, etceteras to do their laundry in my bathroom. This was another mark against him, but again I am kind of tolerant and we had by then been together for a long time. So I again forgave him with a stern warning.

The house had two bedrooms and I slept in one while the other was for visitors. I did not often have houseguests, but one day I looked after children of a friend who wanted a break for a few days. The three boys stayed in the guestroom. It was then I discovered that that room had other, less welcome, incumbents — bedbugs. To those who do not know a bedbug from a bedpan or think that bugs only infect computers, I may tell that they are small insects, which tend to inhabit beds.

They are nocturnal insects like owls, which sleep in the daytime and wait for the dark to emerge from their resting place and bite the unsuspecting sleeper in the bed. They operate like mosquitoes, but more silently and insidiously and their bites itch and itch. If there are many of them, they disturb your sleep and most certainly they are unhygienic although I do not know of any particular disease they infect you with.

We scoured the room, we checked the beds and we threw out three perfectly new mattresses and replaced them. But the bugs kept coming. Then one of the boys woke one early morning and there were the bugs going home for the day. They were crawling up the wall to sleep at the back of the picture rail. One of those old-fashioned bits of wood that were once put round the upper part of the walls of rooms to hang pictures on. That was where the bugs were hiding and we took appropriate action to eliminate them.

But where had the bugs come from? Again it was an unexpected change in my schedule that revealed the truth. I had gone on a field trip, leaving Caleb behind. I came back late at night, instead of waiting to travel the following day. Caleb was in his room, some distance from the main house, so I unlocked the front door and then made a quick check of the house to see all was well.

The check included the visitors' room. As I switched on the light, I saw a row of recumbent forms, some on the beds, some on the floor. In all, I counted twelve men in varying stages of dress, undress, dishevelment and dirt. My visitors' room had been turned into vagrants' dormitory! Or so it seemed. Some, of course, may have had jobs, certainly all had enough money to pay Caleb's fees. I did not scream. I did not call the police. I did not even call Caleb. I felt too tired to deal with him at once. I simply said, "OUT!" And they quietly fled out into the night. I don't know where they went. Maybe they all managed to squeeze onto Caleb's floor. One or two I recognised and was to see again under other circumstances, but most just disappeared.

We had to do the whole bedbug eradication routine again. But again I forgave Caleb, very grudgingly. He was all apologies. It was a time thing. They were all long lost relatives who had come from a burial and he had nowhere to put them. But I was really getting at the end of my patience. Much as I realised that none of us is perfect and that I might get another even less honest, hard working and more greedy and gregarious house servant if I sacked Caleb, I was beginning to think I should make a change.

However, matters were taken out of my hands. Caleb left by himself and not alone, and not without making sure he went with as much as he could without actually stealing from my house.

At first, when I came back from work and found nothing cooked for supper and Caleb absent, I was hardly concerned. It had become his habit for some time to leave the cooking to me and to sneak in at night to eat what I had cooked. Often he would be inebriated from drinking some local brew with his friends outside his house. But when morning came and he was evidently not around, I began to wonder what could have happened to him.

I was not left in doubt for very long. Before I left for work, a large group of his compatriots and drinking companions came complaining loudly and seeking my assistance. Their leader explained that Caleb had absconded with the wife and child of a friend. The whole community was outraged. Not so much because of the wife, but because of the child. They also suggested that he could have taken another friend's daughter whom he had also been befriending. I explained that my concern was Caleb's absconding with anything of mine and clearly the wife and child were nothing to do with me. I was not the deceived husband and father.

They went away abject and arguing. I later discovered that Caleb had gone with something of mine also. Items I had left in the various places where I had been studying habits of the farmers. He had even borrowed from farmers on my account and in my name. So when I went back on subsequent visits, it was to be met with lists of what 'I owed'.

I thought that was the end of Caleb, the inveterate rogue male. But I met him again years later. I was working on another assignment and we had stopped at a small wayside town to buy some refreshments. And there, at the window of the Land Rover in which I was sitting was CALEB!

He acted as if we had parted most amicably. He greeted me as

"Madam" in a most polite manner and asked after the family. He then got to the point. Did I have any job for him? Could I recommend him to someone? I knew how well he could work, after all, he had left without testimonials. Equally politely, I told him that neither I, nor any of my friends had any jobs to offer at the moment. I did not allude to the past. I left Caleb standing in the dusty road, in his patched shorts and rubber sandals, with an optimistic and ingratiating smile. And as I waved to him from the window, I smiled back. Somehow, rogues are not so plausible but so endearing. That is why we always get conned, especially me.

Chained

Monica Arac de Nyeko

On the evening of March 20th 1998, the big bell sounded at exactly 9:30 p.m. This was unusual because it was prep time. We all rushed anxiously to the assembly hall which was lit by a hurricane lamp. Everybody knew it was something very important because assembly was never called that late.

"Attention," Sister John Mary said after everybody had sat down on the assembly grounds. Her voice was shaky, almost crackling to a stammer. I still remember that night. The plants seemed still and the whole atmosphere sinister. All the teachers were there, standing solemnly as Sister John Mary said a very short prayer. I wondered why, because she normally said long prayers, and insisted on saying the rosary. Most students accredited this to her position as Mother Superior of the convent.

"Today's prep ends now," she said and paused. "There'll be no prep on the other days too, until further notice," she added.

Grumbles broke out among the students because we were to write the end-of-month tests the following week. The grumbling didn't last long. "I have very disturbing news for you," Sister went on. "I have been informed, by reliable government sources, that the rebels have planned an attack on our school tonight." She paused, sighed heavily and continued, "Now, I don't want anyone to panic."

The rest of her words brushed by my ears: I began to quiver. There had always been such rumours about the rebels of the Salvation Army Front but none had ever necessitated calling an assembly and certainly, none had ever come true. The enormity of Sister John Mary's revelation shook me. I planned a furtive escape off the school premises.

I had heard horrible things about these rebels and the things they did to people like slitting their lips, noses and ears. I did not want to be maimed. There were also stories about the rapes and venereal diseases. I was not going to stick around to find out if they were true, I decided.

Assembly broke off almost immediately. Everybody went straight back to the dormitories. Activity and movement around was prohibited. All doors were to be firmly locked. Sister emphasised that in case the rebels came, under no circumstances was anybody to scream or panic. Sister would lock the dorms herself to make sure we were safe. I learnt this later from a friend because I was too engrossed in my thoughts to pay attention to all Sister John Mary's words.

I decided this was the ideal time for my escape. I would go in the other direction where I would hide for sometime. Then I would dart off the school compound after everyone was out of sight. Indeed I did exactly that. I sat in a little thicket just around the boundary of the school. I do not know how long I was there because I dozed off a couple of times. After everything was quiet, I sneaked from my hiding place, peered hard to make sure I was not being observed then dashed at the speed of wind. Stones pricked my bare feet, as I panted up the hilly pathway which, unfortunately, I was no match for. The light from a sprinkling of a few stars in the sky and the half-moon enabled me to see a little ahead. The hill ascended further and further and I had to drop to a brisk walk. Occasionally, I heard the grass move, but imagined it might be some bats or rodents disturbing it. I did not know where I was heading to because my home was too far and I had no relatives around. But I kept walking on and on, hoping for some kind of miracle.

"Excuse me," a male voice broke in.

I would have sworn the last time I looked behind there had been no living being in sight.

"Why are you in such a hurry?" he asked softly. I began shaking, my teeth chattered as I stared at him open-mouthed. But I stood my ground, trying to keep my cool. I wanted to run away but, for some reason, did not.

In the dim light, he looked like a boy of not more than fifteen years. He wore a cap and held a catapult in his left hand, which seemed queer. I made every effort not to sound terrified. After all, he was young, so there was no cause for me to wet my pants in fear. From the rumours I had heard about the rebels, I imagined they were enormous, horrible-looking men, with awfully rough faces, almost monster-like. But this particular boy seemed harmless; he looked nothing like the mental images I had formed of the rebels.

I debated whether to answer him or not. Who does he think he is, I thought and said very carelessly, "And you! What are you doing, sneaking up on me? And besides, where are you going at this time of the night and why?" I queried authoritatively after I had convinced myself that he was just a naughty boy who posed no danger to me.

17

"It's only 11:00 p.m.," he said mischievously.

"11:00 p.m. and you're saying it's only?" I snapped.

"Whatever has enraged you, do not take it out on me," he said, offended and added, "In any case, it's you who should be ashamed. No sensible and moral girl should be out this late." He spoke in fluent Acoli, his words too complex for a young boy.

We walked a few minutes in silence.

"Eh, what is a young girl like you doing out here this late, eh?" he teased.

I was beginning to get irritated. I gave him a hard look and said loudly, "The rebels have planned an attack on our school, okay? I am trying to flee." I could not understand my drastic mood swings.

"Oh, so you have come from Sacred Heart?" he asked.

"Yes, yes of course. What do you think? Do I look like a lost pig to you?" I snapped.

"Stop!" he said instantly.

"What?" I hissed.

"I said stop," he barked. "Lift your hands in the air," he ordered.

"Who do you think you are?" I said with a jeer.

He placed his hand in his pocket and pulled out a pistol. "Turn back," he said.

I cannot recall the fear that engulfed me. I had under-estimated this young man. Urine descended down my legs; I was thrown into complete panic. He followed me behind with a pistol held to my back as we headed back the way I had come.

My hands constantly grew tired and sagged. "Straight up in the air," he ordered.

After we had walked a little distance, he whistled. People of all kinds emerged from the bush along the path. They were very creepy. I realised then that I had passed amidst the very rebels I was running from. I began trembling and let out a loud fart for which I got a hard kick on my buttocks. "Stop anusing around," one of the rebels yelled. The rest burst into uproarious laughter while imitating my fart.

The rebel gang was composed of girls, boys, children and fierce looking men. I looked back to estimate how many; they must have been about fifty. They were very organised, doing everything meticulously as if preparing for a very delicate mission, something which puzzled me at the time.

"Stop!" another voice ordered. I stopped instantly. "What's your name?" the owner of the voice asked. He was a tall man, about six feet or more. His hair was dread-locked and fell gracefully over his shoulder.

I spoke very softly, "Ajok. It's Ajok."

"Ajok what?" he asked.

"Ajok Martina," I said.

"Mine is Nyuka-lyet. I am *hot porridge*." He ordered all the other rebels to stand still and gave them instructions. I got my share of instructions, too. The attack was scheduled for 12:30 a.m. that night. From what I assumed, Nyuka-lyet was the leader. I later learnt he was the commander in chief of "Star-grey", a Salvation Army front battalion. It was his group that was to attack my school that night.

"It's five minutes to phase one of our mission tonight, all parties ready?" Nyuka-lyet asked at exactly 12:25 a.m. We waited for sometime for his next command. "Now, proceed!" he ordered, his thunderous voice echoing through the midnight silence. A few minutes later, I was knocking on Sister John Mary's door. Her room was adjacent to the convent rooms.

"Open, Sister, it's me." I said. There was silence for sometime but I kept knocking till I heard movement inside and saw a light.

"Ajok! What are you doing out this late?" she asked as she opened the curtain of her window to peep. She was holding a candle. "I was putting on my veil, I am sorry for the delay," she apologised.

"I was so frightened, so I tried to get away," I began haltingly. "But I had nowhere to sleep, so I came here. I am so sorry, Sister, for troubling you," I ended apologetically. My blood was boiling inside me; I knew exactly what I was doing. The rebels had told me to set her up so that they could carry out their vicious plan. I tried desperately to wink at her. I wanted her to realise something was not right. I even twisted my mouth in a very strange way. She did not see the sign at all. She instead just grinned at me and said, "Stop being comical," as she opened the door noisily and put the candle on the table.

The rebels were skulking about twenty metres away, ready to pounce at her once she opened the door. I had learnt earlier that one of the rebel girls had, apparently, attended that evening's assembly. So they all knew exactly where all the other keys were being kept.

As soon as Sister John Mary opened the door, all sorts of things happened at once. One of the younger rebels pointed a handgun straight into her face, the rest their AK47 rifles. Sister let out a high-pitched sound but silence prevailed within seconds. She must have seen the many armed figures and decided to recoil. The rebels soon had the keys to all the other premises of the school.

"Anyone wants a quick fuck? Lots of vaginas around," Nyuka-lyet bellowed. The boys rushed to the nuns' rooms. Cries of protest filled the air. Even the novices were not spared. One of the boys headed for Sister John Mary, but Nyuka-lyet rebuked him saying, "This one is mine." Turning to me he added, "Come and watch your Mother Superior get holy sacrament." I hesitated a little but felt the tip of his gun just behind my back, propelling me forward.

She was ordered to switch on the lights and take off her veil. She put on the lights but left the veil on as she stood like a hunter with a broken spear before a hungry lion. Nyuka-lyet ordered me to sit on a stool in the corner of the room. Then he shot his eyes at Sister John Mary and said, "If you don't want to take off your veil, I don't care. I will still eat your vagina, anyway. Watch! You may learn a thing or two," he said turning to me.

Nyuka-lyet plucked her veil off with exaggerated force. Her head revealed long, neatly combed Afro hair. He grabbed her by her hair, turned her to face the wall, her upper body leaning over a table in such a way that her lower body faced his directly. Then he lifted up her robe and drove himself very forcefully into her.

I heard a sharp cry of pain from her and I gnashed my teeth. "A virgin at your age! What are all these priests for?" I heard Nyuka-lyet yell, breathing noisily like an ape species. "Are they all eunuchs?" he asked.

I saw Sister John Mary's eyes filling with tears. She slowly turned her head towards me. I still remember the look on her face. Her eyes spoke to me in a language that only she and I could understand.   " You traitor!" she seemed to say and I turned my face away in shame.

As if what he had done to her was not enough, he ordered the boys to carry her outside because she couldn't walk. They crucified her on a huge mango tree right in front of the assembly hall. Nyuka-lyet drew a huge knife from a bag-like trunk he had tied to his trousers. The knife had a blade almost the seize of my two palms put together. He used the knife to rip her robe apart and fondled her breasts a little. Then, in a frightening evil frenzy, stabbed her right between her breasts. Sister John Mary lifted her head in agony and said, "Virgin Mary, intercede for them." Her head fell onto her chest. I turned my eyes away: I couldn't watch any more.

The girls in the dormitory were rounded up and each had to carry a load on her head. They all looked at me like a traitor although I was one of the captives. I had no choice but to lead the rebels to the dormitories and convent. I did not want to die.

On Wednesday by 8:00 a.m., we had walked very many miles. We used the bushy path to avoid possible ambushes laid by government soldiers. Most of us were tired, our feet were aching and burning with unbearable pain. But no one dared complain. Earlier on, one girl had said she was too tired to go any further. When asked whether she wanted to rest, she had hurriedly said yes. She had been cut into pieces almost measurable in kilogrammes.

We came to a river we had to cross. Ten girls drowned. Most girls were in their sleeping clothes, some even in petticoats. Those who tried to cover their breasts were lashed. "Who has never seen those things?" one rebel said.

Another girl swam across, leaving behind a trail of diluted blood-like colouring. "Why did you defile the water with your sins," another rebel asked her. When she did not answer, he pushed her back into the water. He held her head under as she flapped about. Her little efforts to get free were no match for his firm grip. Other rebels cheered. The girl's struggles stopped: she was dead! Her body slowly drifted away with the tide.

None of the rebels touched me. I heard that I had pleased Nyuka-lyet by helping Star-grey accomplish its mission without any hindrance. One rebel girl whose name, I learnt later, was Amito told me I might earn my freedom if I pleased their leader again.

The following day at about 2:00 p.m., the rebels raided a trading centre. They also captured a witchdoctor called Gyerubabel. He was a man of about eighty, flimsy looking and scary. He spoke as if his voice was fading away. He answered all the questions put to him with a certain amount of asperity. This angered Nyuka-lyet and he ordered his shrine to be set ablaze. Fits of fire burnt up the little house, filling the air with a very disgusting smell. Gyerubabel was flogged with bamboo sticks, which landed everywhere on his body. I thought he would fall down and die, but death did not want him yet. Nyuka-lyet got impatient and ordered Amito to hack him to death. She grabbed an axe with the most amazing simplicity and ease and set to work. I bit my lower lip. I wanted to turn away but my head stood transfixed as I watched every moment of it. I still remember the look in Gyerubabel's sunken eyes as he begged her to spare his life. She lifted the axe with all her strength and hacked off part of his neck, leaving the other part sitting loosely on his shoulders as if it

21

did not want to let go.

Blood spurted out of his body from what looked like a tube. The whole sight was frightful. The almost headless body moved about haphazardly till it dropped dead. The commander nodded his head, pleased. Amito dipped her hand into the man's lifeless head, and it came out with blood. She led it to her mouth and licked the blood. I had learnt this was some-thing the rebels did to avoid being haunted by the person they had killed. Nyuka lyet sat silent for some time. He looked at me, studying me as I bit into my raw mango. Then almost instantly, he asked, "Do you want to earn your freedom?"

"Yes," I hurriedly replied. At this stage, I was willing to do anything to be free. I was warned, though, that there was no turning back once I accepted.

"Wait here," he said.

I wondered what was going on in his head, or what I had to do to earn my freedom. I resolved that whatever it was, I was going to do it. He ordered the boys to collect plenty of firewood. They made a very big fire and a saucepan, looted earlier, was placed on the cooking stones. The other girls and I watched the rebels chop the dead body into pieces. The pieces were thrown into the boiling water. The rebels kept whispering to each other and I thought I heard them say, "Let's punish the girls." I tried to avoid thinking about what I was going to be told to do in order to earn my freedom.

After about thirty minutes, Nyuka-lyet beckoned to me. "Get a chunk and eat," he ordered. I froze! He stared at me and then said, "On second thoughts, eat the real Gyerubabel." All the rebels broke into a roar of laughter. I wondered what I had missed.

One boy got up and went to the saucepan. Near it was a metal rod on which was skewed a sausage-like piece of flesh. I looked closer to be sure what it was. Oh my God, I could not believe it! I closed my eyes hard, then opened them. Before me was Gyerubabel's penis!

"Eat!" a voice ordered. My throat went dry when I glanced inside the saucepan and was greeted by another sight. The dead man's eyes gaped at me as if I was his killer. The skin on the body had been scalded by very hot water so that what remained of it was like a shaven sow.

"Eat this!" I heard Nyuka-lyet say again. I will not say how I felt. I took my time, then as if some demon possessed me, I got the metal rod from the young man who held it out to me and bit into the piece. I drove my teeth deep into the skin. The taste was indescribable. I chewed hard as if

I was chewing a piece of rubber band. When I was done, I looked up, tears dripping down my face. "Go!" Nyuka-lyet ordered me.

As I made off, not knowing how I would reach safety, I heard him ask if any of the other girls wanted to earn their freedom. I did not stay long enough to know if they were desperate enough to eat human flesh.

When I was out of sight, I ran at the speed of a whirlwind. My feet did not even feel the thorns in the bushes or the stones that tore at my bare soles. When I thought it was safe enough, I sat down under a big tree. My toes were bleeding and my green polyester dress was torn beyond repair. I sat under a big *kituba* tree and forcefully drove my finger into my throat to throw up the rare meat I had just eaten which sat so heavily inside me, but in vain. I had not eaten the whole day, so naturally my tummy was not willing to give up the temporary answer to its prayer. I cried till my eyes boiled, my mouth dribbled and my head ached.

I had earned my freedom; I thought I was free, but that day, I became a prisoner. A prisoner of my conscience. A prisoner of Sister John Mary's Stare. I am enslaved by guilt of betrayal and other unsavoury memories. I cannot stop hearing those deafening cries of the drowning girls. They haunt me every second of every day. I cannot close my eyes in peace. Meat knows my teeth not. My lips can never tell the story; the story of my treachery. I use ink to atone for my sins. Though I exist, all is futile. I am not free. I don't hope to ever be free. My conscience pricks me every day and I say to myself, "If only I hadn't." But what does it mean, "If only I hadn't — hadn't done what"?

THIS IS MY STORY, THE STORY OF MY BETRAYAL.

Esteri's Secret

Winnie Gashumba Munyarugerero

Joseph Kabuye was a worried man. Worried about his wife, Esteri. For about a week now, she had been acting strangely, very strangely indeed. From the moment Joseph mentioned the plans to celebrate their 25th wedding anniversary, Esteri had become a changed person.

Joseph was now watching her. He was sitting in the main house waiting for breakfast before going off to the school where he had been headmaster for many years. Esteri was in the outer kitchen house, which was directly opposite where Joseph was sitting.

She was sitting with her chin cupped in her left hand, staring into space. Unaware of her husband observing her, she scratched her head with the right hand, still supporting her chin with her left. She continued to look ahead as if her life depended on that one spot ahead of her. The intensity of her faraway gaze was great. She seemed to mutter something to herself and nodded her head.

Her husband, fascinated, watched her every move. Esteri turned her head slightly and the movement brought into focus a hint of a silhouetted outline of the laughing girl he had fallen in love with. A thickness of love engulfed him so strongly that he got up to walk over to her. But he checked this impulse and sat down again. He hated to see her suffer and longed to touch her.

The milk tea boiled over into the open fire and Esteri jumped up as if a bomb had exploded near her. She deftly snatched the hot pan with bare hands from the fire. She licked and blew on the burnt fingers and picked strands of old banana leaves to hold the hot pan with as she poured the tea into the teapot. Once again, she went off to her distant destination. For three or five minutes, she remained standing, her arms folded across her chest, lost in thought.

Her husband, fearing he might have to miss breakfast, decided to disrupt his wife's journey of thoughts. "Esteri, I'm getting late. Will today's breakfast ever come?" he called.

This brought Esteri back from her dream and she picked up the tray. "I'm sorry. I won't be a minute." She carried the tray into the house.

"Esteri, what's the matter with you these last few days? I know you're worried about something. You hardly slept last night. I heard you turning and tossing and this kept me awake. Do you want to talk about what's bothering you?"

"Not now, my husband. Later, perhaps. I'll find a way," she replied, adding the last words more to herself than to her husband.

"You'll find a way to what, Esteri? Is it something to do with our wedding anniversary? Ever since the children mentioned the plans for the celebrations, you have not been the same. You say you don't want us to go to church, but you don't say why. What do you have against church?"

"I have nothing against church. You know very well I love church," Esteri cried out. Her husband looked at her perplexed. "But I'll not go through a mock church wedding. We can have a party here at home or anywhere else you want. There's no need to invite Patrick or Florence," she added with anguish on her face that surprised him.

"I'm sorry I brought this up. It doesn't seem the right time. We shall discuss it later. I hope you'll have found a good reason why my best man and your maid of honour should not be invited to our wedding anniversary." He was trying very hard to keep his voice at normal pitch.

He poured the tea into the cup. His hand was unsteady and the tea spilled over onto the table. He had never known his wife to be so unreasonable. Esteri watched him unnoticed.

He ate his breakfast in silence as his wife sat opposite him, in distant silence. Ordinarily, the two would be talking about one topic or another. Today, not a word was said. Esteri did not normally share Joseph's breakfast but she always sat with him and chatted away. She preferred to eat hers later after her early morning chores of washing and cleaning were done. Which chores she neglected that day. After Joseph left, she remained in the same chair, in the same position for a long time, the faraway look never leaving her face.

"I must tell Joseph. I must. I cannot carry the secret any longer," she declared loudly, at last seeming to become aware of her surroundings. "The weight of it for twenty-five years has nibbled and gnawed away at my soul. I can feel the sore stump sticking out inside me. I will tell Joseph tonight... or perhaps tomorrow. I will not carry this load for another day." She nodded in agreement with her thoughts.

Now that she had decided to speak out, she felt that relief that comes after a long struggle with indecision. But immediately, another hurdle appeared in her path. How was she to tell her husband about what had been locked away in the darkest, deepest cupboard of her soul for twenty-five years?

She considered blurting out the confession, slapping Joseph hard in the face with the truth, straight as it was, following her mother's teaching — "Never compromise the truth and you'll not be compromised." She herself had passed on the same golden rule to her children. She always demanded and expected the truth, the whole truth. She hated circumventing the truth. Yes. She would tell it as it was. She could not bear to live another lie. To stand next to Patrick, before God and the church congregation, and pretend all was well, was something she could never bring herself to do. She would rather die. No. There was no other way. She must tell Joseph the truth about Patrick.

She examined that option — blurt it out as it happened. She rehearsed the opening sentence: "Husband, do you remember our wedding day? Something terrible happened to me that day…"

No. No. That would not do. It would be too cruel on Joseph. It would be too sudden and too shocking. Joseph had been a good husband. He did not deserve to be crushed with the truth. It should descend on him gently and kindly, like a drizzle.

Esteri tried another angle: "That Patrick is a sly venomous snake..." No. That would not do, either. Esteri had been raised to take responsibility for her actions. That opening sentence would sound like she was totally blameless. She was not blameless, she thought. If she was not to blame, then why had she been burdened with the millstone of guilt all these years? If for nothing else, she was guilty of keeping her husband in the dark all these years.

"Oh, if only I had told Joseph earlier!" cried Esteri. She tried two or three other opening lines and rejected them all. They all seemed inadequate.

Finally, after a long battle, she settled on writing her confession in form of a letter. On paper, she could describe her feelings uninterrupted. She could pause to search for the right word. Talking to Joseph face to face on such a matter would be hard. Her husband still intimidated her at times, when he asked questions. Some of his questions were difficult to answer because they required one to describe one's emotions. Oh, why do I always find it hard to describe how I feel, she groaned hopelessly. I want Joseph to understand how much I have suffered all these years. Face to face, I will not find the right words. On paper, time is on my side.

I will write Joseph a letter, a long letter telling him not only what happened that happy day-turned-tragic, but I'll also tell him how I have felt ever since.

Filled with this new-found resolve, Esteri immediately got up. She almost ran to her room, so light was she. She dug some money from her savings to go and buy a sheaf of paper and a large envelope. With quick steps to keep pace with her determination and relieved tension, she stamped her way to a nearby shop. She purchased five sheets of the kind of paper that is actually two sheets in one, not cut but joined. Those are ten sheets, twenty sides. That should be enough for what I want to say. If need be, I'll come for more, she told herself as she handed over the money to Karoli, the shopkeeper.

Karoli wanted to talk but Esteri cut short his attempts, much to his disappointment. Today, Esteri was not in the mood for village gossip. Karoli looked at her quizzically and considered her behaviour rather brusque.

Once home, Esteri settled down to pour out her heart to her husband, so as to purge her soul and let him know why she was against Patrick's involvement in their wedding anniversary celebrations. She began:

My dear husband, I am writing this letter to tell you what I have wanted to tell you all these years we have been married but lacked the courage to do so. Now I must, because I cannot hold this secret any longer.

Many times I wanted to confess. It was always hard. I did not want to hurt you or risk your anger. As I write now, I am praying that you will understand how I have suffered carrying this load. Read what I have to say and decide what to think of me.

You know I have always tried to be open in all my dealings with you. Yes. I tried to be as open as was humanly possible, to make up for the secret I harboured. My guilty conscience was striving to ingratiate itself.

For you to understand, I must go back in time to bring nearer highlights of some events in our lives.

You remember how we met. I was a young woman training to become a teacher at Zzaana T.T.C. You were then teaching at Zzaana Primary School. You were, by far, the most handsome man on the entire hill. I still keep those passionate letters you wrote to me. They showed you as a gentle, sensitive and kind man. I loved you completely.

I vividly remember the time you proposed to me. The very words you said are forever engraved on my heart. Even before you said anything, I sensed you had an important announcement to make. You were very nervous but also excited. You must, of course, have had no doubt that I would accept you. My feelings for you spoke loudly enough for the deaf to hear and the blind to touch. My love was that obvious.

Then when I took you home to meet my family, you were an instant hit with my mother. I read her approval in the glitter of her eyes the moment she saw you enter the room where she was sitting. Her whole face lit up as if someone had turned on a light switch inside her. As for my father, true to his African culture that despises a show of emotions, he wore a hard face. But I knew him too well to be deceived. I could see that he, too, liked you. Beneath his toughness, was the most kind-hearted, generous and loving man I ever knew. I still miss him very much.

How I have thanked God a thousand times for that first time our bodies united as one! At the time, I thought it was a weakness on our part, especially mine. I had so much wanted to keep my purity to my wedding day. I am so glad you took that purity when you did. You argued that after paying the bride price, I was all, except in name, your wife. What remained was the Christian formality of a wedding in church. In truth, the burning desire in my body consumed me. I am eternally grateful for that moment of weakness.

Then our wedding day came. It is one day I want to remember, yet one I long to forget. In part it was the happiest and yet the saddest day of my life. One moment I was floating high on the air of happiness, the next I sank to the depth of despair and filth. One moment I glowed with beauty, the next I felt dirty and ugly beyond description. I have tried to wash and scrub away the filth but after twenty-five years, I still feel the remains of dirt inside me. This is the reason I must describe to you what happened on our wedding day. You will also understand why I have vehemently and consistently stated that I can never have Patrick re-enact his role as your best man on our twenty-fifth wedding anniversary celebrations.

You came to our home with your chosen escorts. In the midst of music, dancing and feasting, my father handed me over to you. I will not try to describe my feelings because I cannot find the words. I felt that a difficult task had been finally accomplished.

For me, the climax came when my father, with mother smiling with delight beside him, handed me over to you. The church provided an occasion for dressing up, but little else. My bridesmaids, certainly, enjoyed the show. The droning of the old priest made little impression on me, so much so that I can hardly remember a thing of what he said. As far as I was concerned, I had already given you my body and soul.

After the church ceremony, the photographs, the congratulatory embraces and hugs, it was time to make the seven-mile journey to your...our home. Your party had mobilised bicycles and motorbikes. The bride took the place of honour on Patrick's motorbike. You, the maids and the guests were to follow on bicycles.

You remember you had arranged with my aunt Birungi to prepare for our stopover. She was to receive me and entertain me while we waited for the rest of you. Then the procession would, after refreshments, move in one body for the short distance to your home.

I was gently propped up on the seat of Patrick's motorbike. You instructed him to ride at a slow speed and not to fly as he usually did. For some short distance, he rode slowly but increased speed as we rode along. The whistling air did not allow for much conversation. Only a few sentences were exchanged.

At Mabunga, Patrick turned into the footpath to Mabunga Primary School. I was surprised. I tapped him on the back to find out what was happening. He continued as if he had not felt my inquiring fingers. I was thinking hard. Where were we going? Why hadn't you included that bit of the journey in your instructions to Patrick?

He rode past the primary school and went uphill to the little church. As you may recall, the church was then just a simple structure. It had a door-way and openings for windows but there were no door or windows to shut. It was wide open. It was many years later that the original structure was enlarged and doors and windows fitted.

There was no furniture in the church, only papyrus mats on the floor. People in those days carried chairs from their homes to church on Sundays. School children carried benches from their school below.

Well, at the church Patrick stopped, got off his motorbike and helped me down. He must have seen my worried and questioning look but he avoided my eyes and ignored my questions. He left me standing outside and entered.

Church is supposed to be a place of tranquillity. But an eerie feeling of foreboding pervaded the atmosphere at the church that Saturday. Just as I was about to take off and race down, Patrick, who seemed to guess what I was about to do, roughly grabbed me and dragged me into the church. By now I was screaming for help. But even as I screamed, I knew it was useless. On a Saturday afternoon in the month of December, when schools were closed for holidays, there was not likely to be anybody around. We had seen nobody at all as we rode past the school.

Patrick flung me down and charged on top of me like a bull on heat. I was too shocked to know what to do. Before I collected my wits, he had tossed up part of my bridal gown to cover my face. He ripped my under-clothes like a crazy dog ripping meat off a bone. Frantically and blindly I fought with all the strength within me. The devilish Patrick had care-fully planned his crime. He knew there was no help. I fought blindly and as I could not see Patrick's face, I ended up hitting air with my fists. I could sense the murderous savagery in his whole being. He was not a human being. He was a hungry lion grabbing and mauling to satisfy a greedy hunger.

After his heinous act, he watched with glee as I tried to cover my nakedness. He said — I can still see his face and feel his scorn — "You dare not say a word of this. Your sweetheart may not enjoy my leftovers. It is in your best interest that no one hears of what has taken place, least of all, your Joseph. You have everything to lose."

But I did tell my aunt. How else would I have explained my weeping and the dust that covered my wedding gown? My aunt seemed to share Patrick's view. She warned me not to utter a word to you or anyone else about the incident. I would gain nothing, she warned me.

She cleaned me up as best she could and bathed my face swollen with weeping. She urged me to put on a smile for you when you arrived. The smile pasted on my face was so forced that the facial muscles ached.

Joseph, your friend raped me. There, on the church floor, in the house of God, in my wedding gown, that beast tore me apart. I felt filthy then. I have felt filthy ever since. How can such a beast act as your best man again? I would rather die than go through such a ceremony. Have I not suffered enough having to smile and be nice each time he called on us? And why do you think I refused to have him as David's godfather? That devil is not fit to be anybody's godfather or even earth father. He should burn in hell!

Now you can begin to understand my strange behaviour during the days and nights that followed. I hope you can appreciate why I cringed and froze each time you approached me. I saw the image of Patrick in you whenever you came close. It was only your love and gentleness that restored my womanhood.

That, my dear husband, has been the bitter and ugly part of my life I had hidden. With the celebration of our twenty-five years in marriage coming up, I could not go through it with my burdened soul. And cer-tainly, not with Patrick next to you as the best man! Thank God he works far away in Tororo and has not been seen around in many years. His *absence at the occasion will not raise any questions. Our people have a saying that a child that plays with his excreta soils himself with it. Let us not play with any excreta, Joseph.*

Your wife,
Esteri.

PS: I think it is best that I should be away when you read this letter. I am travelling to my mother's place. I'll stay with her until I hear from you. I shall willingly return when you signal me to.

A Job For Mundu

Jackee Batanda

Mundu swiftly wiped sweat from his endlessly perspiring forehead with his hands. As he stood on the pavement outside Cairo International Bank on Kampala Road, he cursed the gods and everyone else responsible for his predicament. Fate seemed to have joined arms with his enemies to mock his every effort to succeed in life. He turned and looked into the glass that graced the bank. For the first time, he saw himself as he really was, a twenty-eight year old second-hand coats and shoes hawker.

He had been in the hawking business for eight years and this was going to be his last day. The business had its good and bad aspects. His clients, as he preferred to call them, came from all walks of life: the minister, in his glamorous office, and the wheelbarrow pusher from Owino Market. He prided himself in having everything for everybody. His mobile *bend-down* boutique ably competed with the uptown boutiques. There was no difference in the merchandise. They included designer names like Louis Vuitton, Calvin Klein, Gianni Versace…the entire lot of them.

Mundu spied a sleek Mercedes Benz parking in the bank's parking lot. A minister glided out of the car and went into the bank. Mundu swiftly looked away to avoid making eye contact with him. He knew *Mugagga* (rich one), all right. He had sold designer suits to him many times. Only yesterday he had been to *Mugagga's* office and had sold him the suit he was now wearing as he strolled into the bank. The driver, as usual, had come for him from Amber House where he usually stood with his merchandise. He had been chauffeured to the office. The *askari* had let him go in without going through the security checkpoint. Who would dare disturb the visitor of the 'honourable-minister-sir'?

In the office, *Mugagga* had waved him to a cosy leather seat. His poverty-shrivelled buttocks had perched where richly endowed ones had sat before. He had smiled to himself as he always did when he sat in the plush chairs.

"What do you have today, *Mutembeyi?*" *Mugagga* had asked. 'Mutembeyi' was the local name used for hawkers.

Mundu, assuming a servile expression, had replied, "*Mugagga*, I have chequered jackets and square-shaped shoes. The latest on the market."

"Show me." *Mugagga* had nodded in appreciation as Mundu displayed his wares. "These are good. Has anyone else seen them?"

"No, *Mugagga*. Your eyes are the first to feast on these jackets and shoes," Mundu had hurriedly answered as he had already told five other 'Mugaggas'. It was a game of survival.

"How much are you charging?" *Mugagga* had asked.

"The jacket goes for forty-five thousand shillings only and the shoes for thirty-five," Mundu had quoted humbly.

"You are expensive, *Mutembeyi*. It is like buying from the shops!" *Mugagga* had exclaimed as he usually did when trying to intimidate Mundu into lowering his price. But Mundu no longer felt scared. He was used to *Mugagga's* antics.

"Eeh... *Mugagga*, the prices in the shops have gone up. Look at my jackets," Mundu had said, holding out one of the jackets for *Mugagga* to see. "First class, *kabisa*," he had declared looking *Mugagga* straight in the eye. The rich always try to haggle the already low prices. "The dollar keeps rising, pushing up our prices." *Mugagga* had paid half the amount without blinking an eye. He had bought three jackets and two pairs of shoes.

"I will give you the balance next week," he had said putting away his newly acquired stock.

"Thank you very much, *Mugagga*," Mundu had said, as he quickly stashed the money out of sight before *Mugagga* could change his mind. As he turned to go, *Mugagga* had called him,

"*Mutembeyi*!" Mundu stopped dead in his tracks. "Just one more thing."

"Yes, *Mugagga*?" Mundu had anxiously replied.

"You have never seen me, except in the newspapers that litter the streets of Kampala," *Mugagga* stated matter-of-factly.

"Of course..." Mundu hesitated, then added, "*Mugagga*, I don't even know where your office is located. Seeing you is like trying to see the President. *Mugagga*, I swear on my grandmother's grave I have never laid eyes on you in my short twenty-eight years on this earth."

"I was just checking. Keep it that way." *Mugagga* had waved him out of his office, satisfied that his little secret was safe.

Mundu had left the office pondering over the unpaid balance. Getting the money out of *Mugagga* was not going to be easy and yet he was planning to leave the business. He had worked with these people long enough to know how they treated their creditors.

Mundu was shaken out of his reverie when his colleagues swiftly picked up their wares and scattered in different directions. The shoes that had graced the pavement had disappeared into thin air. The pavement was now clean. Mundu turned just in time to see the Kampala City Council henchmen jump off their trademark green pickup. He quickly joined in the game of hide and seek, darting between cars as he ran for safety. He saw an unlucky hawker grabbed and thrown onto the back of the pick-up, joining the unfortunate groundnut and envelope sellers squashed in the corner. He ran and disappeared into the crowd of onlookers.

These were some of the things he was tired of. The time of playing hide and seek was over. This scuffle was the last straw that convinced him beyond all doubt that it was time to leave the streets and get a permanent job. There had to be work somewhere and he was going to find it. The best employers were the *Wazungu* (the whites) because they paid well and if one was lucky, he was showered with goodies. It was also said that when they were leaving, in most cases, they left the houseboys with their household property. He had to find such a job and settle down. Mundu was through with the life of haggling with customers over even the lowest prices. It was time to change.

Traversing estate after estate was not what Mundu had envisioned when he left the streets to look for a stable job. He had thought that jobs for *shamba* boys and house-helps were not going to be difficult to find. Three months had gone by and he was still without a job. Frustration had started to get the better of him. The hope he had cherished three months earlier was waning.

Moreover, when he had gone back to *Mugagga's* office for his balance, *Mugagga* had called a policeman to throw him out, threatening to have him arrested, if he did not stop harassing him for money. Mundu had not believed the threat but when he had gone back, he had been locked up in the basement for over three hours and continuously tortured. The memories suddenly came back to him as he stood in front of a high black gate.

His hair was now ruffled and he wore a dirty shirt. Standing outside the gate, he suddenly became conscious of his appearance. As he held out his right hand, preparing to knock, he hesitated and told himself that this would be the last home to visit looking for a job. He was going to give up and go back to the village if he failed this time. 'Lord, let it be the last home I knock at,' he mumbled as he feebly knocked at the gate.

An *askari* opened the gate immediately as if he had been waiting for the knock.

"Can I speak to the Madame?" Mundu asked.

"What do you want?" the *askari* asked.

"I am looking for a job. I was wondering if the people here have work."

"Wait here," the *askari* said, locking the gate. He trotted off to the house. Mundu waited for a long time. When he was about to lose patience, the *askari* came back. "Come this way." He led Mundu to the front of the house without another word. Mundu was presented to the mistress of the house.

"Good afternoon, madam," Mundu said when she appeared.

"Good afternoon," she replied. "How can I help you?" she asked, looking him up and down as she dropped into a garden chair.

"I am looking for work," Mundu replied looking down.

"Where have you been working?" she asked, looking at him through her eyelashes.

"I have been hawking things to people but the business is tough. KCC has been harassing us, so I want to change and work for a salaried job."

"What can you do?" she asked as she filed her nails without looking at him again.

"I can do anything," Mundu eagerly replied. "I can wash clothes, cook food, slash the compound and any other work you may have for me." Excitement made him talk rather fast.

"Go slow!" she barked. "How much would you expect to be paid?"

"Twenty-five thousand per month" Mundu said.

"Twenty-five thousand!" the woman of the house exclaimed.

Mundu was alarmed and hurriedly interjected, "Okay, I'll work for twenty." At that, she raised her eyebrows.

"ll work for fifteen then …ten…," he continued reducing.

The shocked woman of the house said, "You can't work for ten thousand shillings a month! I was just shocked that you can ask for so little. I'll take you on for thirty thousand shillings…." She paused, then added, "but first, I'll talk to my husband. Wait here." She stood up gracefully and walked to the house. She spent quite sometime away before she finally emerged, accompanied by her husband. Mundu froze in shock at the sight of the man. The same reaction was reflected on the man's face. The husband was no other than the 'honourable-minister-sir', *Mugagga*.

Out Of The Trap

Ayeta Anne Wangusa

They met on a lonely path. His glittering pupils behind his thick lenses frightened her. She lowered her eyes. Her heart was trembling beneath her chiffon blouse. Darkness was rushing in from behind the hills; running after the big orange sun. She said hello and passed by hurriedly.

She recalled this encounter, deep into the night, as she lay in her ragged nightdress, while the world went to sleep. She did not care about the layers of cloth that cushioned her, because she felt God had been careless with His hands when He moulded her. She felt that no cloth from the market could hide the navy blue pigment on her forehead that made her feel ugly. Her dwarfed pride had been kicked about like a fibre ball in the red earth, until she transformed into a snail, hidden in its shell. She recalled, from inside her shell, how many of her colleagues at school used to mimic the way she spoke, like an African parrot. When she was younger, her siblings rolled the shell round the house with their bullying feet, until her mouth smelled of silence.

So she lay on her bed listening to the butterflies dancing in her stomach, as she thought about Daudi. She drifted away from this pleasure and decided to have a heart to heart talk with God: "Father, you gave me everything but a face. When I open my mouth to speak, I think everyone will laugh at my voice. I begin to shake like a leaf, when I see all the eyes pinned on the navyblue birthmark on my forehead. Oh Father, let me talk to the world like I talk to you."

Time came for her to go to secondary school. She went to a day school in Kampala. Her father, who lived in Lugazi, handed her over to Kaloli, her cousin, who worked in the city, and begged him to take care of her school fees and accommodation. Kaloli had a two-roomed house. She slept in the living room, he in the other room. She rolled her mattress up during the day, hid it behind the door and let the room wait for visitors.

When she walked out of the door to go to school, she withdrew deeper into the shell as the new world greeted her. But the neighbourhood did not see the navy blue pigment on her forehead. The teenagers noticed the swollen flesh around her nipples. They noticed that the left swelling was bigger than the right swelling and they ran home to ask their mothers why. They realised that her hips gave her straight skirt a wide succulent shape. They peeped into the shell and admired her shinny dark face. They approved of the innocence seated in the white pupils. All of them concurred that she was chaste, and nodded in unison that she would make a good housewife one day.

She did not notice them. All she saw was the man who greeted her along the lonely path. The man she could not talk to freely. The man she was infatuated with. She lay on her bed in her ragged nightdress and extracted the words she used to speak to herself. She carefully arranged them in a row on the page of her mind. She then began to mark different words with the stroke of her invisible pen; the words she would use the next time she met him. Was she in love with him? She was not sure. Daudi had tried to chat her up before, but she did not know how to respond to his charm. So she acted awkwardly. Running past him and reminiscing about him when she rolled out her mattress to sleep at night.

On her way to the market the following day, along the lonely path, she walked with her eyes focused on her toes. She did not like her toes; they were not shaped like Milika's. But she could not hide her toes in her Bata school shoes because Kaloli insisted that she wears slippers while at home. There was no money to buy a pair of shoes every term, so he reasoned.

She had unconsciously developed a stoop, her eyes studying her toes because whenever she walked to the market with a basket in her hand, the boys in the neighbourhood ran from their homes to the dusty road to feed their eyes on her. She did not understand why all of a sudden she had become their centre of attraction. Yet when she was younger, living with her parents in Lugazi, the boys in the village had kicked her about and curved out her stoop. She was now a snail that trailed the lonely path with its shell on its back. If only they saw my crooked toes, they would run away for life, her inner being would speak.

Daudi often met her on the lonely path as she walked to the market and created small talk. He asked about her family, her school and how she was. On this particular day, when she bumped into him on the lonely path, she realised that there were no more words between them. She gathered motion in her body ready to slide past him, to continue her trail, dragging her shell on her back ... but he held her arm and whispered in her ear that they should meet. Some place, somewhere.

"When?"

"Tomorrow."

"Where?"

"Under the mango tree near the church."

"Time?" she was almost soprano with thrill.

"7:30 p.m." Daudi's deep bass made spasms of excitement run through her whole body as she found her way to the market. The two new lovers dispersed in a hurry.

So she was standing next to the mango tree near the church the following day at 7:30 p.m. The wind was blowing so furiously that she thought about the village ghost who took evening walks in such hideouts. "Oh my God, where is Daudi?" Her heart started thumping when she saw the thick black clouds gathering over her head. Then lightning slashed the sky and it bellowed in pain. The cry sank deep in her stomach and she could not bear the waiting any more. She started for the foot-beaten path that led to the church and almost bumped into a tree trunk that stood in her way.

It was Daudi coming up the hill in long strides. "Where are you going?"

"I thought you weren't coming," she said, looking at the mourning sky. Raindrops from the heavens began to soak her face. She felt the butterflies in her stomach seep into her knees when his strong arm was wrapped round her waist.

He walked her back to the churchyard, where he was sure nobody would notice them. It was very dark and even the two new lovers could not see each other's face. She found herself leaning on the church wall, while her breathless lover stood in front of her, almost engulfing her petite body with his wide chest. He touched her in places where her hands had never reached. Her head was running away from her body, leading into her wild dream hidden at the apex of her head. She did not know what to do, what to expect. She just stood there as he sought her lips in the enveloping darkness. It was now drizzling.

The shell rolled off her back as she released a weak cry from deep inside her and threw her arms in the air. Like a melting candle, her body slipped out of David's firm grip, flowed to the ground where it solidified at his feet.

"What is it?" Daudi asked as he followed her to the ground in panic. He thought she had fainted. She had expected him to lift her from the ground with his strong arms and lay her on the moist grass. She had wanted him to continue the journey of his hands to the place where her hands had never been, while lying on the moist grass.

Daudi's eyes waited for an answer. He waited for her voice to reassure him of life. She did not respond to his question because her cousin and guardian, Kaloli who had stalked her to the churchyard, suddenly popped out of his hideout when he saw her melt onto the ground. His swollen jealousy could not allow him to suffocate a cough that was grating his throat.

The two new lovers did not wait to identify the cough of the intruder that sprouted from behind a tree trunk. They dispersed in different directions. Daudi joined the village road and curved his way through the hasty crowd that was running away from the frozen raindrops falling out of the sky. Nakku ran to her home, her dream shattered.

Kaloli walked home after her. He did not reveal his identity as the owner of the cough that had sprouted from behind the tree. He ate the food she had prepared for supper in silence and retired to his room. Nakku rolled out her mattress on the floor and lay down to sleep in their small sitting room. She tried to think of her Daudi, but the cough that had germinated from behind the tree trunk haunted her. She closed her eyes and wore her shell like a hood.

She met Daudi once again. He was in a hurry. Did not want any interruption this time. He ate her voice with his mouth. It was a painful and short time. Pain, little tears and blood. Kaloli was peeping again.

"I saw you with Daudi," he rushed to her when she dragged her dusty feet into the two-roomed house. "You've been at it again. This time I have to tell your father about this. You are shaming our family."

"You won't...please don't," she pleaded, bending her bruised body, almost kneeling down.

"I will, you can't stop me."

"I will give you anything that you ask."

"Oh, how generous of you! Let's do what you've been doing with Daudi."

"No!"

"Why not?"

Silence.

"Well, you had better make up your mind before I tell your father about it."

"Tomorrow then."

"Deal."

She could not hear of her father knowing about her little sin. He had told her to behave while under Kaloli's care, for he was the one who held the key to her education. She had to obey Kaloli or else she would end up like her primary schoolmates who had already become wives back home in Lugazi. Wives because their parents did not have enough money to keep them in school. Her family was blessed to have Kaloli working in the city. So she had to commit another sin to seal Kaloli's lips for life.

Lying on her bed at night, Nakku could see her father's teeth crashing her in his mouth after learning about her corroded hymen. She could feel the pain of her bones cracking, grinding, pounding under her father's breathless fury. So she gave in to Kaloli's lust, so that he could keep her little secret.

Knock, knock, knock.

"Who is there?"

"It's me." Who else could it be? She hated her body. She was angry with herself. She was outside her shell.

Kaloli's hot body appeared at the door. "Why so early?" he asked, his eyes burning the remnants of her self-esteem.

"Is it the time that matters?" she asked, her anger bursting out her. "I have to go to school." She wanted to seal his mouth as soon as possible.

Kaloli's mouth contained stale slimy saliva. His hands were rough. His heart was cruel. He made his way into his treasure but found another man's footmarks deep in the cave. Kaloli sprang away from her body, as if a bee had stung him. He did it to spite her. But she was outside her body. Her soul asleep.

"You are so cheap! How could you? Your father has to know about this," he threatened her.

"But you can't, we had a deal. Besides, I would also tell father what you've done to me," she argued.

Kaloli's cynical smile spread across his face before he said, "He would-n't believe you. You are my cousin, remember?"

Nakku grabbed her clothes and dressed in a hurry. She walked to the door and asked, "What do you want from me?"

"Let's do it again tomorrow," Kaloli stated coldly.

She let his stale mouth and rough hands visit her again, to keep her little sin with Daudi concealed from her father. Her body and soul began to accept Kaloli's rough hands. She had to stop seeing Daudi. She felt too guilty about her relationship with Kaloli to continue seeing Daudi.

But someone was watching her. Sanyu had seen her closest friend coil into a shell and had wanted to know why. Nakku could not open her mouth. When Sanyu insisted, she burst into tears and ran home to grab the mattress from behind the door. She lay down and wrapped her sore heart with sleep.

It was after a week that Nakku unwrapped her heart from deep inside her and presented it to Sanyu. "I've been having an affair with my cousin and now I am trapped."

The confession struck Sanyu like a bolt of lightning. She tried to compress the pain carried in the news that her friend was telling her. How can I comfort her, she wondered. "Nakku, you should not have let this happen to you. You should break free from this cycle. This is incest!"

Sanyu could not conceal her anger. But Nakku was happy that she had got it off her chest. She was confident that Kaloli would no longer continue blackmailing her with Sanyu at her side. She felt her self-esteem return when Sanyu cursed Kaloli for bullying Nakku into having sex with him.

When Kaloli crawled back into Nakku's bed next time, he found that Sanyu had breathed life into her. He found an energy that was so hot, that for the first time, he looked for her voice in her eyes.

"Remember our deal? You give it to me or I tell your father."

"I'm not your whore anymore! You can go and tell my father, if you want. But I will not have your slimy body crawl into my bed again."

Startled by her outburst, Kaloli said, "Now you think that my body is filthy after I have protected you from your father's wrath!"

"You have not protected me from my father. You have used me. You have used me..." Her voice was thinning like the hair of an aging man. Nakku began to cry. She began to weep like a woman who had lost a child from her womb.

Guilt started chewing at Kaloli's soul. He had never seen Nakku like this and he knew that if she cried louder, the neighbours who lived in the semi-detached houses would want some answers. So he walked over to her, and gathered her into his arms. Her heart was falling out of her body, through her mouth. It was the silence that had been trapped in her mouth. Now it was falling out of her mouth. Noisily. She tasted her salty tears, travelling from her eyes to her mouth. This was the pain of her incestuous relationship with Kaloli. The more her voice fell out of her head, the more she tasted the pain of her life.

Kaloli tried to soothe her. He kissed the salt that flowed from one eye. Then he tried to drink the pain that flowed from the other eye. But he found that Nakku's heart was no longer trapped in her mouth.

She screamed, "No!"

"Come on, Nakku, don't attract the whole neighbourhood. I'm only trying to help."

"You are not trying to help anyone. You only want to boost the fire of your lust. Get away from me."

Kaloli tried to trail his rough hands between her thighs, but Nakku was ready for him. She pushed him hard against the wall and kneed him right into his incestuous balls. It was time for his voice to fall out of his mouth. He cupped his hands so that his voice could not drop to the ground and crash. Crash with a thud so that the neighbourhood would run to see what was amiss.

Nakku kneed him into the balls a second time. His eyes did not have tears. His eyes did not carry pain from the past. They were an empty dam. This time he covered his mouth with his cupped hands and ran out of the room.

He run out of her life and she walked out of his life and started a new life as new as a young banana tuber. Fresh and succulent.

***

...And all who had kicked Nakku about in the red earth when she was younger, stood at a distance — and looked. They were amazed to see her walk with her back curled-out-straight, with her eyes looking confidently to the future. The snail in its shell was gone.

Raindrops

Mildred Kiconco Barya

I peek at the silhouetted figure etched against the wall. The orange sunset fades from view. The mind seems in some kind of neutral state to ward off psychosis. A thin line preserves sanity from utter madness. Empty existence. Hurt is in the silence that crams the air. A wordless atmosphere.

The elements gather their force. I can feel a storm brewing. Thunder rumbles in the sky. Blinding torches of lightning split the environs. Clouds begin to congregate. Turbulence swells. A fear churns my stomach lining and tears through my throat with a mild groan.

"Oh Lord, does he know I am here?"

I move resolutely through the evening chill and approach him. At the nearness of determined footsteps, his face turns. The jolt of recognition slows my pace. I stop, suspended. The paralysing question hangs unuttered.

His chest seethes with resentment. His hardened heart blames men and fate for all the misfortunes.

The painful memories bounce back in queue. Frightened eyes blaze with fire, the cynical mind set against a cruel world. The wounds on the inside hurt, inch by inch.

We were walking the same road. We built a dividing wall. We forgot the thrill of being alive.

He stares straight into my eyes and his lips crack into a well-rehearsed, detached smile. No words, no reason bigger than life, no place beyond the now. Hollow laughter hides the mute cry. I turn to walk away, headed, who knows where.

"Tanya!" he whispers my name. "Come back."

The clouds above are very heavy. A choir of wind begins to hum the notes softly, and then it whistles and eventually breaks into a song. The leaves on the trees turn their cups to the skies in expectation. Generous raindrops begin to fall, welcome as light after the darkness. They melt the barriers at last. Nothing rivals the sight of us held in a sweet embrace.

Miss Nandutuuu

Beverley Nambozo

"Good morning Miss Nandutuuuuuuu!" the class chorused.

I really disliked the way the senior twos prolonged the last vowel of my name as if it was a piece of chewing gum whose elasticity they were measuring. Was it because I was a new teacher? I had thought coming back to Makerere College where I had been a student would have been more rewarding than this. In those days as a student, I was rarely teased. Students had treated me like a wild flower that was supposed to be looked at with curiosity but not touched or smelt. It had paid off because I rarely got involved in student wrangles and managed to pass my exams well.

"N-N-N-Now..."

"Haaaaa!" the class shrieked. My stammering problem was just getting worse.

I continued, trying to raise my voice above the din. The Dean for lower school, Mr. Tumwebaze passed by. Why did his office have to be in such close proximity? I pretended not to notice him standing by the window as I commenced with my English lesson. "Somebody read the title and first paragraph," I ordered.

David Kiyingi, the class captain, offered to read. "Countable and Uncountable Nouns," he started.

"Countable Nouns are those that c-c-can be..." The class burst into fresh fits of laughter. Tears pricked my eyelids. I did not stammer through any fault of my own. Why couldn't I be confident like my friend Janet, who was so affable you hardly noticed her stammer? She just went on and on like a parrot that one felt almost intimidated by her affability. She actually left you feeling worn out. I also had an albino friend, Simon, who had many friends in spite of the fact that many students and other people, for that matter, fear albinos because they do not understand why they look different. Anyway, he had an amazing ability to make friends and had been the first student from the school to participate in the Regional Inter-school Sports competitions. Was that how one arrived at such confidence? Did it mean that I had to acquire a special skill to be taken as normal? And it was worse when even the class captain participated in tormenting me and sat back mocking me with the rest of the class.

The Dean was still standing by the window. He was wearing a grim expression when I turned to face him. He told me that he would see me during the lunch break.

I felt so unfairly treated at the way he summoned me to his office like a puppy. A lump rose in my throat almost choking me. I quickly scrawled down some homework for the students on the chalkboard, scraping it with my fingernails in the process. White chalk dust rose and entered into my badly manicured nails and comfortably settled there. I became more flabbergasted. The class started to stifle giggles but one look at my stern ashen face silenced them. I had stomached enough of their nonsense for one day. It was a shame that it was only on such rare occasions that they kept quiet.

The bell for the end of the lesson went. I gathered my books with so much force that I caused more white dust to rise and make me cough. And with as much dignity as I could muster, I marched out of the classroom straight to the staffroom. I tried to ignore the rude stares from the other students that I passed. So what if I looked like a white and black version of a Ugandan teacher? Was it my fault that chalkboards were the most affordable means of teaching aids?

As soon as I got to the staffroom, I slumped onto a chair. The usual hustle and bustle typical of break time helped me escape from my present problem. Cleaning the chalk off my face and hands, I made a beeline for the huge kettle of tea, which had been prepared from the boilers in the smoke-filled kitchens.

"Will you please pour some tea for me?" one teacher asked.

"And me too," said another and another until I was pouring steaming tea for everybody into the chipped flowery designed mugs that Makerere College could afford to give to staff. I smiled at the lady who usually brought in meat samosas. She actually made them herself. And although I personally felt that they were just small half-ready meat samples covered with a thin film of very oily yet burnt pastry, I still went ahead and bought them.

Break was always a hurried affair. Much as students were usually punished for getting into class late after the lessons, even the teachers needed a little reprimanding. Most of them made it just in time after standing outside the classroom doors wiping oil away from their mouths with their handkerchiefs that substituted the chalkboard dusters. The beginning of such lessons usually commenced with meat particles darting out of the teachers' mouths onto the books of unsuspecting students.

The bell for the end of break rang and I inadvertently got a patch of milk tea down my red quilt teaching attire. "Sorry, sorry," the guilty party muttered while spitting milk tea into my black glossy hair that still had chalk dust in it. The other teachers followed suit and grabbed chalk before dashing out for their lessons, for which they were already five minutes late. At least I was free until lunchtime. And that was the time Mr. Tumwebaze was going to talk to me.

Usually, in my free time, I designed my lesson plans or read the papers. But right now I could only think of what that the Dean was going to say to me. This was not the first time he had found me teaching a rowdy class. The last time had been the worst: the class had refused to answer any question I asked. When I told one of the students to stand up, he pretended to be deaf. I had been previously warned of stubborn students but not of completely horrible and unbearable ones. My hurt was their joy. They knew I hated it when they made noise in class but just went right ahead as if it was a contest for the fittest vocal cords.

Anyway, I knew for certain that I did not hold a very good record with the Dean. Could the Board of Governors have held a meeting to discuss me and decide to make me resign? What if I quit first and beat them to it? I had failed to get a grip on the classes I taught. Maybe teaching was never meant for me. Maybe I should teach deaf children? I had also failed to get a grip on the cane. That smooth piece of bamboo that was meant to discipline and teach African children. I could never understand how the other teachers, especially the one in-charge of external affairs, could get the cane and bring it down onto the buttocks of a child without flinching.

I remember an incident when I had caught a child with a caricature of Mr. Tumwebaze and myself in a very suggestive sexual position in the staff room. The teachers told me to punish him, so I did exactly that. The naughty student's name was Bob. He was a typical senior two student with shabby hair, unpolished shoes and a rubberband at the end of a stick for a catapult, which he safely kept tucked in his torn grey socks.

"Bob, do you promise me you will never do such a thing again?" I asked.

"Yes, madam." So I punished him by making him apologise to the staff, which he did humbly and I let him go. An apology in front of the staff was one of the worst punishments that I could think of.

Unknown to me, though, no sooner had he left the room than his friends, who appeared from nowhere, started to give him pats on the back for surviving the cane. The other teachers immediately called him back and told me to cane him.

I remember holding the cane, and just as it was about to reach its destination, fate would have its way and I gave a long sneeze. *At-t-t-ishooo! A t-t-t-t-ishooo!!* I remember the silence that descended on the place; a silence that was almost as thick as well-cooked *posho*. And then, as if the Owen Falls Dam had been given a go-ahead to start operating, the room filled with raucous laughter.

From that day onwards, I was known as the teacher who not only stammered in speech but became a bundle of nerves when it came to punishing students as well.

Tears pricked my eyelids once again, as I recollected all this. I decided to walk out of the staffroom at this point and pretend to be making a call on my mobile phone. Holding back the rest of the tears was proving difficult. It was like holding back water running freely from a tap. The mobile phone did not seem to help.

The remaining hours to lunchtime passed quietly because I did not want anything or anyone to jostle my already disquietened spirit. The clock ticked on slowly, emphasising the emptiness in the staffroom. The sound it made was like a stone dropping from a quarry onto the ground below, causing an echo as if to remind its environment of its short time of existence.

When the students finally came out in small groups with worn looks on their faces, shirts untucked and socks down to the ankles, I knew it was lunchtime even without hearing the bell ringing.

Of course the first person that walked into the staff room was Mr. Tumwebaze. I had never come to terms with calling him by his first name, Samson, like the other teachers.

"So, Miss Nandutu," he began in his condescending voice, "what happened? And this is not the first time!" His middle finger was wagging at me like he was lecturing his puppy for wetting the house. It was actually his engagement ring finger that he was wagging. He often used it in rebuking students. The engagement ring flashed at me. Mr. Tumwebaze was engaged to a born-again Christian girl. I heard he had met her on his ranch in Western Uganda.

Mr. Tumwebaze did not even have a mobile phone, so that story of his ranch was highly doubtful. The ring was made of copper, which he claimed was cut from Zambian copper and had been bought from the National Museum.

As he waved it at me again, the afternoon sun reflected on his suspenders that holted his big rolling stomach from rolling off his body. The thought of his stomach rolling off his body, like a football, made me smile. Mr. Tumwebaze looked at me in disbelief but I could not stop giggling. At last I managed to stop. And then a big hiccup came out of my mouth, startling me - *Hiccup!*

The other teachers started to come in, one by one, for lunch break and could not understand why Mr. Tumwebaze was looking at me with a stern expression while I hiccupped away. I stood looking at him with a helpless expression, waiting for my dismissal. *Hiccup!*

"Ma -Ma-Ma- Miss Nandutu! Um-Um…!"

That was the last straw. Now Mr. Tumwebaze had also started stammering like me. I laughed the more and when he opened his mouth as if to say more, my only response was a loud - *HICCUP!*

Headlines

Hilda Twongyeirwe Rutagonya

His name was flashed on all the news headlines. Ian Butetere's face glared on all TVs and newspapers. All radio stations screamed 'Ian'. That had been Ian's dream. To make headlines! His mother had told him that he had been born great. So he tried to live great and hoped that he would die great.

As soon as Ian learnt the meaning of the phrase 'news headline', he took interest. Every time he glanced at a newspaper or listened to radio or TV news, he would catch himself fantasising about his own name, Ian Butetere, being flashed as a headline. God knew what Ian wanted and he graced him with keenness to know more. From day one when Ian stepped into the classroom, he never went beyond the fifth position. Some day I know I'll make it, he always thought with a sparkle in his heart.

It was a season of warmth as graduands-to-be criss-crossed streets, opened and closed door after door, calling on their friends and friends of their friends, or their parents' friends and brothers' and sisters' friends to contribute to the noble cause of graduation. Ian had come to one inevitable conclusion: he was not going to fundraise for any graduation party. He had only a handful of friends and distant relatives in Kampala. Even those, he had noticed hurtfully, had started dodging him, not wanting to be bothered. There was no point in having a lousy party that would cause blisters to his soul.

Ian had one kind distant uncle — Uncle Tobi, who had agreed to stay with him after university till he found a job. Tobi and his wife, Stella had even agreed to prepare a small dinner party for him where a few people would be invited. Tobi was from Ian's mother's clan and Ian had come to know him from his mother. "He's a very good man," his mother had insisted. "Go and seek him out, my dear. He will give you drinking water in Kampala."

"You don't know those Kampala people, girl," Ian had replied. Ian called his mother 'girl' as an endearment but her real name was Joyisi.

"No I don't, but I know Tobi. He is my brother. His grandfather and my grandfather were so close that at times they brewed sorghum beer for each other and slept in each other's home, drinking."

At his mother's insistence, Ian had eventually sought out Uncle Tobi who had welcomed him into the family like a long-lost son.

Tobi was a driver with the National Water and Sewerage Corporation. Once in a while, Tobi would give Ian a little pocket money to assist him in his search for jobs, but on many occasions, he walked the streets. He was amazed at the numerous little corners that hid inside the shell of Kampala, which he had not discovered during his stay at the university.

"Uncle Tobi," Ian said one morning as Tobi handed him transport money to go and do an interview, "the day I get a job, count my first salary as all yours."

"By the time it comes, you will have a thousand and one cares that you will either have forgotten about your pledge or pray that I forget about it," Tobi replied, laughing.

Ian did several interviews without success. "Have you left money for processing the shortlist?" one secretary had asked him as he walked out of the interview room. "Have you left tea for the panel?" another had asked. "Have you brought a sample of what you take for breakfast in your home?" He had been asked such and several other questions that he had almost given up the hope of ever getting a job. Then one day when Uncle Tobi returned home from work, he handed him a khaki envelope. In one corner of the envelope were the words, 'If undelivered, please return to: God Sent International, Box 17, Kampala'.

"Who the hell knows me in God Sent International?"

"You should be telling me that."

"Now, I remember. God!"

"Anyhow, stop giving your girlfriends my address," Uncle Tobi joked and watched Ian greedily tear at the envelope, his hands shaking. Ian drank in all the words and finally looked up at his uncle who was still standing over him. Uncle Tobi opened his eyes wide to meet Ian's. Ian then nodded his head and the two smiled in mutual understanding.

"When do you start?"

"One week after graduation."

"Working terms?"

"Godsend, Uncle Tobi."

"I'm so happy for you, my dear son."

"Thank you."

"Do you remember you almost gave up?"

"The false competition. I was getting tired. I told you about the boys who came for that interview. They were all driven to the venue and they all looked at me as if I was scum. As I walked to them, holding an envelope with my documents, they looked at one another and quickly covered up the space that remained on the bench. Fine, my shoes were dusty and my shirt stuck onto my clammy back, but they had no right to treat me like that."

"No, they did not."

"If it were not for you, I would have given up the hunt. Thank you, Uncle Tobi."

"Well, all thanks go to the man above."

" I don't refute that but he acted through you."

"Pleasure. So, how do you intend to spend your first salary?"

"I don't even know." His uncle looked at him jolting him into remembering his promise of a few months before. The two laughed hilariously and locked their hands into a vigorous handshake. Ian felt like he was being welcomed into manhood.

As Ian waited for graduation day, which was a few days away, excitement began to build inside his every nerve and tissue like a tyre being pumped. He ticked off each day on the calendar that hung above his bed.

One week to graduation, Ian woke up in high spirits. He was going to pick his graduation gown, hood and cap. As he walked to Makerere, a fierce exhilaration engulfed his whole being. He was going to graduate. He was going to wear that magical outfit. He was going to be photographed and his pictures hung in their house in the village for all visitors to view. His mother was coming to Kampala to attend the graduation ceremony of none other than her own son, Ian Butetere whom she knelt down and delivered. He felt like the highest tree branch, listening and dancing to the tune of a soft wind. His lips tore into a huge grin and he felt his insides jump up and down.

"Hi!" a former classmate reached out for his hand.

"Eeh. Charles, I did not even see you. How are you?"

"Fine thanks. I thought you were smiling at me! How are things?"

"Not bad. And you?"

"Okay. My dad just got me a job with Save the World International. And you? Any chances yet?"

"Yes, I got a job with God Sent International."

"That is something! Congs," Charles said as he grabbed Ian's hand for a handclasp. Not just something, Ian thought but the words 'thank you' formed on his lips and he voiced them then wished Charles a good day.

Ian hurried towards the main building. A newspaper vendor dashed to the taxi that had just stopped near Ian. More students who were also coming to clear with the University jumped off. The vendor waved the papers.

"*Agalelo! Agalelo*," meaning the daily newspaper. As usual, the headline attracted Ian. "FROM GUTTERS TO STATE HOUSE!" Ian wished he could read the story there and then but he knew he had to wait for the evening when Uncle Tobi came home with a copy of the office paper. Other students joined Ian. Laughing heartily and updating one another on recent events, they filed into the main administration block, emerging later one by one each bearing the degree attire. Ian hurried home to prepare for the journey to the village to collect his parents for the graduation ceremony. But on his return from office, Uncle Tobi told him that it was not safe for a *mugole* to travel, and instead sent his son, Kareb.

The eve of graduation was full of excitement. The air, too, seemed excited as it turned out unusually hot. Parents and relatives of graduands arrived aboard upcountry buses and taxis. Ian's parents, too, arrived with two big cocks and a sack of Irish potatoes.

"Girl, I should take you round the city before you go back to the village."

"Yani, you will take your father, not me. Not among these cars I've seen following each other like sheep filing out of their sleeping quarters. No."

Joyisi called her son 'Yani' not as an endearment but because she had failed to pronounce the name 'Ian' properly.

"I'll make sure you're safe."

"No. Do you want me to die before I return to Bufundi to tell stories from Kampala? You will take us around when you buy a car of your own. And in any case, I only came for our graduation."

"Your graduation? You and who?" Ian's father asked Joyisi. She felt a storm build up inside her, but she fought against it, not wanting to spoil her son's happiness.

"Hmm! You have asked me," she responded quietly.

"Didn't I hear that Mondo's son has two cars?" Ian's father turned to him in an attempt to avoid the embarrassing response from Joyisi.

"Hmm," Ian responded, not making it any easier.

The conversation suddenly stopped. The three of them never managed to sustain a conversation for long. Mother and son never quite felt that husband and father was part of them. What right has he to ask me about this graduation, Joyisi fumed silently and her mind plunged into the past.

***

Ian got his name from a white man who came to Bufundi sub-county to teach women about family planning. Ian was not born yet but his birth was due. Many women, Joyisi inclusive, gathered at the sub-county headquarters to listen to the white man. His name, the sub-county chief said, was Ian Blake. The women heard Yani Buleci. After the seminar, the women returned to their respective villages. Later, Joyisi felt pains attack her stomach. She tried to sleep but failed. She quietly walked around the house, taking care not to wake the children. She felt so cold and went to the kitchen to light a fire. In the dead of night, the pain intensified so much that she could no longer bear it silently.

"Call your grandmother," Joyce shook her eldest daughter, Flora awake.

"Who?" Flora asked, sleepily.

"Kaaka. And hurry." Grandmother came hurrying behind Flora, supporting her frail back and legs with a bamboo stick.

"Joyisi," Kaaka called, peeping through the door. "Hmm. The baby is coming. I can smell it." She hobbled out of the house and returned with a calabash of green liquid she had squeezed out of leaves. "Drink all. And do not breath in-between if the medicine is to work." But the water was so bitter that if Joyisi had dared to breathe in-between, she would not have managed to drink it all. As she handed the calabash back to Kaaka, more pain clutched at her lower abdomen, spreading to the lower back. She bit into her lower lip and firmly held the middle pole that supported the kitchen. A small cry escaped her mouth and Kaaka told her to shut up.

"Don't you dare! Don't you know that if you cry the baby will die?" Joyisi wondered whether the old lady still remembered how birth pangs felt. Before she had enough time to get angry with her, another wave of pain reeled through her whole body, compelling her to push.

"You have delivered him, my child," Kaaka said, holding a little brown being that had popped out of Joyisi at supersonic speed, leaving her stomach sagging like a sack just emptied of sweet potatoes.

"Joyisi, you have produced a king, my child. He is in a net."

"What?"

"Look." A thin membrane covered the baby's body. Kaaka made a small tear with her fingernail at the baby's forehead and the membrane disappeared instantly. She went on to wash the slippery creature when

53

she realised that its left hand was bunched into a fist.

"What are you holding, my little 'husband'?" Kaaka asked the baby, whose toothless mouth kept twitching up and down as if in answer. "Open your hand and share with your wife," Kaaka continued to speak as she gently forced open the delicate hand.

"*Abungura ba Kagunga ka Mutegire ya kinama! Yamawe!*" Kaaka swore, holding the little hand open.

"What?" Joyisi asked, startled by Kaaka's swearing.

"It's your son. I told you you have delivered a king. See this?" Kaaka said holding up the boy.

"He looks okay to me," Joyce replied looking up at him.

"What looks okay?"

"What did you want me to see?"

"Pumpkin seeds. Here," she showed Joyce the cream, seed-like small structures that lay on the palm of the baby's hand. "These are pumpkin seeds. Your son was born in a net and now he's holding pumpkin seeds. He will grow up to be an important man in society. He has come with his own riches. Call his father. He has to witness this.

"Don't bother," Joyce remarked.

"Don't be selfish. Let him share his son's luck."

"He's not in the house. He has not returned yet."

"From where? It is coming to morning."

"From Nnalongo's bar," Joyisi said, trying not to sound angry.

"That *Malaya*! May that drinking place be struck by lightning! And you, my grandson," she said, turning to the baby, "you are welcome to this family. But you must not grow up to be as useless as your father." She wrapped him in Joyisi's old skirts, and laid him next to her. In the morning, the women whom Joyisi had been with at the white man's seminar came to see her and said that it was the white man who had brought her good luck of a perfect delivery that night.

"What was his name again?" they asked.

"Yani Buleci."

"Yee! This little thing should be called Yani Buleki."

"He will be Yani, yes, but the other name is Butetere because he was born with pumpkin seeds."

From then on, the baby came to be known as Yani Buleci, later changed to Ian Butetere. Ian Butetere grew up to see less and less of his father who had almost got married to Nnalongo's bar.

Joyisi worked in other people's gardens to feed Ian and the other children and to get their school fees. Several times they would be sent away from school for non-payment of fees. In their homestead, salt was a rare delicacy. They ate food with salt only on Sundays and other big days like Christmas, but Joyisi never gave up. Unfortunately, for one reason or another, these children did not all continue in school.

Ian had four brothers and three sisters. He was the last-born. Not because Joyisi could no longer bear more children or was practising what Ian Blake had taught them, no. It was because after Ian was born, his father became a total drunkard. He slept in the bar, and the few nights he was at home, he would be so drunk that he would remain in a drunken stupor and fall asleep in that state until morning. She tried to complain, but as time wore on, she gave up the idea and later thanked God for this inadequacy, as a measure of family planning. Ian grew up to be very bright. And he worked so hard if only to please his mother. She was his mother, his father and his friend. Due to long spells of absence of the father, Ian shared his mother's bed longer than the other children.

It was no wonder, therefore, that Joyisi saw the son's graduation as the sky, which they had together touched.

***

Before Ian went to bed, he ironed what his parents were going to wear for the ceremony. He also ironed his suit, which Uncle Tobi had given him. It was Uncle Tobi's old suit but it looked new. After buying it, he had put on so much weight that he had failed to fit into it after donning it only a few times.

Uncle Tobi's National Water and Sewerage Corporation Toyota pickup was cleaned and it shone like a black stone in the early morning sun.

"I'll drive your parents there first because they need to sit in the shade. If they arrive late, they will have to sit behind where there's no shade," Uncle Tobi said to Ian who was busy preparing himself.

"And if they sit behind, they will not be able to hear my name being read."

"True. So I'll come back for you or you could hurry and come with us. But that would mean you would sit on top of the pickup."

"No. Take them while I complete dressing up," Ian said to Uncle Tobi. I have always moved on top of this pick-up and was grateful for it, but not today, he thought.

"I hope you'll be ready when I come back," Uncle Tobi said as he drove off with Ian's mother and father.

Ian was ready long before his uncle came back. He stood outside the gate and waited, watching vehicles drive past. He stood with his head held high and his heart swelling with bliss. Standing there, dressed in the black elegant gown, the stylish black cap with red strings dangling and the double coloured hood, he felt like a multi-coloured butterfly swimming high above the rest of humanity. He glanced at his watch and hoped that his parents and uncle were safe. These road accidents are a menace, he thought, as he adjusted his cap.

A car passed by and somebody waved to him. He did not recognise him but somebody else in the same car had caught his attention. Is he pointing at me, Ian wondered. As he tried to relate the faces to people he knew, an IFA vehicle appeared following as if in hot pursuit, roaring like Karuma Falls. One of the faces of the passengers in the first car then concretised in his memory. He had seen him at God Sent International, one of the boys who had denied him room on the bench to sit as they waited to be interviewed. Ian smiled in triumph, but the feeling was short-lived. The IFA was approaching so fast and Ian noticed that its movements were zigzag. He jumped and ran towards the gate but within seconds, there was no distance between him and the concrete fence that surrounded his uncle's house.

***

"Before we proceed with the ceremony," the Vice Chancellor bellowed in the well-set microphones, "let us all stand up and have a moment's silence in honour of one graduand, Ian Butetere, who has just been hit by a fast running vehicle. May Ian Butetere's soul rest in eternal peace."

"Amen," everybody responded except a few parents and guardians who did not understand English, Joyisi and her husband inclusive.

Hardly twenty minutes later, Ian Butetere's story was selling like hot cakes. All media stations were sending out news-reporters to gather as much information as possible.

"Stay put," they all promised, "as we get to you more news about the graduand who has just been hit by a fast running car. It's not yet clear whether there is any hidden motive behind the accident." Each station boiled with excitement, sending on air the most up-to-the-minute information.

Only this time, Ian was not able to listen to or read the news.

Hard Truth

Lillian Tindyebwa

I could not believe any of the things they were telling me. They brought me to this hospital and insisted that I was mentally disturbed. Nobody seemed to understand me or tried to. If only they could get to know that I was only trying to come to terms with the shock realisation of who I was, and that it was not easy for me.

When I arrived at the hospital, a doctor came to examine me. He said he was Dr. Bernard. I did not like the way he carried on as if he had answers and solutions to everything.

"Hello, Elizabeth, how are you feeling today?" he beamed. His voice sounded as if he was speaking from a thousand caves and the echoes were deafening. And instead of helping me, he was giving me a splitting headache.

"Go away," I screamed, holding my hands to my ears. "You are not my father! You don't even know him or me. And how I feel is not your business!" I kept on screaming. Then I felt hands holding me as I tried to get up and run away from the place.

I do not remember clearly what happened after that. It seems I slept for a long, long time. When I woke up, there were two nurses near my bed and the doctor was gone. I liked the nurses. They reminded me of my mother. She was a nurse and she used to look smart and knowledgeable in her uniform. She probably is still a nurse. Right now, I am not sure what she is or what she is not. I was told that when I fell sick, I never wanted to see her.

There was a small, dark nurse that chirped like a bird whenever she brought me medicine. And I had made up my mind that Miss Bird was not going to give me any medicine. Every time she came in, I pretended to be asleep and nothing would make me wake up. Then she would go and call a certain fat nurse whom, for some reason, I would accept the medicine from. But I would swallow the water without the medicine, which I would keep in my mouth and spit out later when she left!

Well, that was three months ago. Now I am quite used to Dr. Bernard. Even his voice sounds almost normal. He tells me that my improvement

57

is remarkable, and that if I keep taking my medication, I will be out of the hospital in a few weeks. He has also been taking time to talk to me and has asked me many questions about my life. This is what I have been telling him:

I grew up with my mother whom I loved very much but from about the age of four, I developed an obsession of wanting to meet my father. It started in nursery school when other kids would be talking about their daddies. It hit me hard that I could not offer stories about my daddy. Every time I visited my friend Titi, I always wished I could be like her. Her father would always take us whenever I was with her to visit interesting places. Sometimes, he would play football with Titi's brothers, Jimmy and Kaka who were about eight and ten years respectively.

For some reason, I never talked to anyone about my secret wish. I never told my aunt Rachael, my mum's sister or uncle Biti, her husband. And above all, I never asked my mother about my daddy. Even at that age, I had this feeling that she would not like to be questioned about him and probably one day she would tell me without my asking.

My mother was a nurse. She was, therefore, transferred to different hospitals from time to time. But by the time I was about eight, I noticed that her transfers were too frequent. This unusual frequency of transfers meant that I had to move from school to school. I came to resent these movements. Time with good friends was always so temporary and leaving them was always hard and painful for me.

When I was eight years old, I also noticed that my mum did not look like a happy person. I never saw her laugh like Titi's mother used to do. She laughed a lot with her friends and her family. But mum always just smiled. I always wished she could find something to make her happy like Titi's mother.

A couple of years later, she seemed to change, though. She could laugh and be very talkative after taking some bottled stuff which, I came to know was liquor. Well, if it could make her happy, I had no problem. However, as time went by, she would take the liquor and lose control of her faculties. On several occasions, she failed to get to her bed. Then I, together, with the maid, would struggle to carry her to her bed. I came to learn, later, that this also affected her work. Many times, the hospital matron found her sleeping due to a hangover or actually drinking on duty.

This also contributed to her numerous transfers as each administration always wanted to push her elsewhere. She was lucky that she was not actually sacked. One day, I decided to talk to her about reducing her drinking. So when she came from work one evening, I sat with her and I said, "Mum, I was told that alcohol can cause illness. So I thought I should tell you about it."

"Who told you that? I hope you have not been talking to people about me," she said almost angrily.

"I cannot talk to people about you. I only do not want to see you ill."

"Thank you, Elizabeth, but you know I am your mother and I know better what is good for me. I am also a nurse, so I know all about illness," she said agitated.

"But maybe you can just reduce so that you do not fail to go to your bed at times," I pleaded looking at her. She stared back at me angrily, but I so much wanted to tell her all I had, so I continued, "You know, even the maids keep leaving us because they get tired of having to carry you to bed. And, Mum, I fear you might lose your job if you..."

"Enough, Elizabeth!" she shouted before I could finish. "Since when did you become my advisor to tell me what I can and what I cannot do? You don't respect me at all."

"No, Mum, that is not true," I said, feeling worried by her anger.

"Shut up, young lady, and stop telling me how to live my life!"

"Mum, I am sorry but I was only..." At that moment, she moved swiftly from her seat and came and pulled me up and slapped me hard. I screamed, thinking that it would scare her but instead, I incensed her even more. She rushed outside and picked a very big stick and beat me up thoroughly. I screamed and begged her to stop but she seemed to have lost all her senses. "Mother, please," I cried out, "forgive me please... please don't beat me..."

Eventually, she stopped but from that day, our relationship changed. Beating me became her second pastime to drinking.

With this turn of events, I started thinking of my father even more than ever before. I had always conjured up very fantastic images of what my father must look like. I always had a picture of this smartly dressed or suit-clad figure driving an expensive car and living in a posh place. I always imagined how he would come to take me to visit him during holidays or coming to visit us wherever he could. I believed that if I found him, I would ask him to advise my mum on many things.

When I went to secondary school, my life became a little better because I was then in a boarding school. Although I was always worried about my mum, I enjoyed being at school. But when I was in senior two, I came home for the second term holidays only to find mum packing. She had been transferred once again, to Kago Hospital.

At the new place, we unpacked and started arranging things. As usual, other hospital staff came in to greet us and get to know us. They came one by one or in groups. I was always impressed by the kind of reception people gave us wherever we went.

Later that day, in the evening, when I was helping the maid to prepare dinner, a man came in, alone. He was of medium build, dark, and must have been handsome when he was young. He was wearing a black Tee shirt and a cream jacket. I could tell he was a selective dresser.

The maid let him in and called my mum who was busy tidying up her bedroom at that time. When she entered the sitting room and saw him, she hesitated at the door and I saw her face change. But she quickly regained her composure and said, "Oh Dr. Bengo, we are happy to see you! What a surprise after all these years!" But I could tell there was no happiness in her voice as she talked.

"I am happy to see you too, Olive, after all these years." She moved towards him and they shook hands. She did not sit down immediately but remained standing for some time as they talked. I thought this unusual. She eventually sat down.

"What brings you to Kago Hospital?" she asked Dr. Bengo.

"I work here, Olive. I came here six months ago and I head the Orthopaedic Unit," he answered.

My mother looked like she was hit by a snowball. "So we are together again," she said at last, sarcastically.

"Together yes, I mean working together again," he added as if to make sure she understood exactly what he meant.

'That's fine," she said curtly and kept quiet.

"Take it easy, Olive. I just came in to say hello to a fellow staff. I'll go away again."

"Take it easy indeed! Things are always easy for you, Joseph Bengo. Easy to break off an engagement without an explanation! Easy to turn up again as an old friend after all these years."

"Oh Olive, it wasn't easy for me either. Look at it objectively, please, what option did I have?"

"Option? Did I have an option? Was it my decision to be raped?" mum screamed.

"No, of course not. But try to see it my way. How could I marry a rape victim and bring up a child of a rapist? No, Olive, I had to be true to my feelings and leave you to cope as best as you could. And I am happy to see your daughter has grown up…"

"Dr. Dengo, you are the most despicable and heartless man I've ever come across!" my mum hissed, staring at the man who had once been her fiancé. "You are the lowest form of a human being. You are…" she paused as if searching for words. "You are not even fit to be called human because your utterances just now show that you lack basic human qualities," my mum added standing up. Her eyes had turned red with anger, the way they normally did when she was about to beat me. I shivered.

"I can see you are still the same old Olive," Dr. Dengo said with a sneer, "overreacting unnecessarily. All I said was that I was happy to see your child has grown up in spite of her unknown paternity…"

"Enough, Dr. Dengo!" my mother shouted. "And don't talk about my daughter. You left us long ago. You have no right to walk into my life and open old wounds. Just leave us alone - now! I don't want my daughter to see you." But in her anger, mum had forgotten that I was in the next room and could easily see and hear everything that was going on in the sitting room. I don't know how I got the courage, but this was not the kind of thing I would keep quiet about. I walked into the room. I did not want that man to leave before I gave him a piece of my mind.

"Mum," I started, "do you have another child?" She looked at me and then at Dr. Dengo. She sat down and started sobbing.

"Mum, please answer me. I need to know who this child of a rapist is?"

"Elizabeth, please, this is none of your concern," Dr. Bengo said.

"Tell me the truth, did you break off the engagement to her because she was raped?" I shouted.

"Elizabeth, it was a long time ago. We had just been making our plans for the traditional introduction. I left her at 9:00 p.m. and later that night, thieves broke into her house and attacked her, raped her and stole her things. I was devastated of course but, Elizabeth, I really could not…"

I did not hear the rest of his story. I yelled and fell on the floor. When I came back to my senses, I was in the hospital. I have been in and out of hospital ever since. Now, I know this will be my last time in hospital. The truth is hard for me, but now that I know, the cross I bear will be lighter.

Stepdaughter

Deborah Etoori

Monica met Jack at a party organised to bid farewell to her uncle who had been a headmaster of a privately owned school. It was an excellent school, which attracted children of wealthy people. After a brief introduction, Jack and Monica discovered that they were both students of Makerere University and had a lot in common. They stayed together for the rest of the evening. By the end of the party, they had exchanged telephone numbers and promised to keep in touch.

On reaching his room, Jack sat at his study table to study but could not concentrate. He decided to go to bed but failed to sleep. He kept remembering the short time he had shared with Monica that evening and felt a strong desire to hear her voice again. So he went to the booth and called her.

"Hello, Monica," he said. "This is Jack. I just called to say that I enjoyed your company very much at the party and to find out if you got back safely."

"I did, thank you and goodnight," Monica said.

Two days later, Jack called Monica again and asked her out to dinner. She accepted his invitation and they had a pleasant time together. They felt at ease with each other as if they had been friends for a long time. When Jack escorted Monica back to her hostel, he asked if he could see her room.

"No, Jack, not this late at night. But on Saturday afternoon, Jane, my classmate is coming for some discussions. You are so well informed, why don't you join us? It would be nice."

"I would like that,' Jack said.

"Good. We will meet then and Jack, let's just be good friends, okay? I don't want to do anything that both of us would regret in the future, if you see what I mean."

"Yes, Monica. I understand and I respect your views."

And so it was that when the two of them met, they confined themselves to discussing various issues that kept their relationship on an even level.

Occasionally, they attended church service together, went to a movie or a dance on campus and Jack always dutifully accompanied Monica back to her hostel. Gradually, they became quite attached to each other. Neither of them would go anywhere without the other, although at the same time, they never lost sight of the boundaries they set themselves at the beginning.

One weekend, Monica wanted to go home and invited Jack to accompany her.

"Are you sure it will be okay? I don't want to get you in trouble with your parents," Jack remarked.

"It will be okay. My parents and I understand each other well. I take my friends there often, but you are the first male friend I am taking to them. Usually, the boys I go with are relatives."

"Thank you. I shall be honoured to meet your parents."

Monica's parents were middle class. Her father was an under-secretary in the Ministry of Local Government and her mother was a State Registered Nurse. She telephoned her parents and told them she was going to visit them on Sunday and was bringing a friend with her.

When Monica and Jack arrived at her home in Mukono, Mr. and Mrs. Kityo, her parents, were waiting for them. Monica's younger brother and sister, who went to day schools were also there. They received Jack like an old friend and made him feel at home. He and Mr. Kityo talked about various issues and got on well.

Meanwhile, in the kitchen where Monica was helping her mother with lunch, they talked about Jack. "Thank you for bringing us a visitor. We love visitors and he is a pleasant young man. I don't seem to have seen him before, who is he?'

"He is just a friend. We met at uncle Mulinde's farewell party and we have been friends since."

"You have never brought a boyfriend home before, are you serious about him?"

"We like each other, that is all… so far."

"Remember you have to finish your studies," her mother warned.

"I know that, Mama," Monica replied rather shortly.

"All right, I know you are a sensible girl and won't put yourself in trouble. Let's serve lunch."

After lunch, Jack and Monica left the jolly family and returned to campus. "You have a wonderful home, Monica. No wonder you go there so often," Jack remarked.

"Mm, I love home. We are all a bunch of friends, and are open with each other."

"No secrets?"

"No secrets."

"You are a lucky girl."

Time went fast with classes, studies, assignments and eventually, examinations. One year after they met, they both graduated. They organised their graduation parties in such a way that they did not coincide and each could attend the other's. Monica went to teach at the school where her uncle had been a headmaster but she lived with her parents. Jack got employment in an engineering firm. They continued to see each other often, especially on weekends when they could go for a drink or a movie.

One day Jack asked, "Would you like to come and see my people next Sunday, Monica?"

"Why, yes. I think I would like that," Monica replied after a brief hesitation.

"That is nice of you. Shall we go to the eight o'clock service at All Saints Church and go home after that?"

"That will be fine. Let us meet at the western wing of the Church."

That Sunday, after the service, they walked down to Kampala Road from where they boarded a taxi to Makindye where Jack's family lived. When they arrived at Jack's home, a plump three-year old girl shot out of the house and came running to meet them while chanting, "Daddy, daddy, daddy."

Monica was lost and she shot an enquiring look at Jack. Jack scooped up the girl and hugged her lovingly. He then answered Monica's silent enquiry, "This is my daughter, Mabel. I will explain later."

"Obviously you cannot explain at this moment," Monica observed curtly. There was pain in her voice.

"Take it easy, Monica. I promise I will explain."

Now, what have I got myself into, Monica thought. There was a lump in her throat, as if she wanted to cry.

They entered the house. Jack's parents, Mr and Mrs Musoke, were in the sitting room. The father was reading *The Sunday Vision*, while the mother was reading *The Sunday Monitor*. They both stood up to receive Monica. The mother hugged her perfunctorily but there was no warmth in the gesture. "It is good to meet you, Monica. We have heard a lot about you from Jack. Welcome to our home."

"Thank you, Mama," replied Monica.

The father extended a strong handshake, "Welcome, Monica, make yourself at home."

"Thank you, *Taata*."

Monica was lavishly entertained. Mrs Musoke had a housemaid, so Monica did not have to go and help with the cooking. Instead, they all sat and talked over drinks. But Monica was uneasy. She kept looking at Mabel, who, she noticed, resembled Jack very much. The whole family seemed to dote on her, which did not make it any easier for her to like her. What happened to her mother, she wondered silently. Why did Jack not tell me of her existence all this time we have known each other? Monica longed for the visit to end because she was not enjoying it. She was preoccupied with these questions about the child and could not rest until she knew the answers. And yet, this was not the time or place to demand for answers. Jack noticed her despondency and tried to draw her into conversation without success.

Mabel, on the other hand, was forthcoming. She sat near Monica and showed off her toys. "Auntie, look at my dolls' house. Granny gave it to me," she told Monica.

"It is a very nice house. Where are the dolls that live in it?"

"I am going to bring them," the child said, jumping up.

"Mabel, don't trouble aunt. She is too big to play with dolls. Take your dolls' house with you," Mrs. Musoke snapped at her.

Monica sank deeper into her misery. She could not understand Mrs. Musoke's resentment. Was she, perhaps, a good friend of Mabel's mother? But where was the mother, anyway, and had Jack married her? Is he a widower? Many questions were spinning in Monica's head to which she wanted answers.

Mr. Musoke spoke naturally, unaware that there was anything wrong. But Jack, watching Monica closely, was very much aware of her discomfort although there was no way he could help her without making things worse.

Soon after lunch, Monica excused herself on the pretext that she needed to go and prepare her lessons for Monday. After farewells, Jack and Monica started off. "Daddy, are you coming back soon?" Mabel asked Jack.

"Yes, little one, very soon."

They walked silently for some time. "Thank you for inviting me. It was good to meet your parents and Mabel."

"They have been expecting you for some time. I talk about you quite

65

often," Jack said. Before entering the taxi, he added, "Let us go to Makerere and sit somewhere and talk."

"All right, but why Makerere?"

"I don't know any other place with plenty of space to sit and talk."

They headed for Makerere. There was little talk in the taxi. There they found a secluded spot under a tree and sat down on a bench. Here they could talk undisturbed.

"Monica, there is need for us to talk about Mabel."

"Us? I don't know anything about little Mabel, so I have nothing to say about her. You are the one to talk about her."

"Hey, hey, that is not your usual tone. Why are you sulking?"

"I am not sulking. I am just shocked that all this time we have been together, you never told me you had a daughter!"

"Monica, having a child out of wedlock is not something one easily talks about. To be honest, I feared that if I told you before we were stable enough, you might have walked out on me. I would not have endured that. I love you so much."

"Love does not go together with secrets."

"I know, but try to see my predicament."

"I feel like a silly girl who has been flirting with somebody else's husband."

"I am nobody's husband. It was just a silly mistake, which I honestly regret. We were not even in love or thinking about marrying. She is now happily married to another man. But the child is mine."

"Mm, so you are probably hunting for a mother for your daughter. Cross me off your list. I would not like to get into a situation where the first child I have to look after is a stepdaughter."

"Please don't call Mabel a stepdaughter. When I get married, I expect and hope my wife to treat Mabel as our daughter, not a stepchild."

"Whether you like it or not, this dear, sweet child will always be a stepchild and she will only have a stepmother and stepbrothers and stepsisters."

"At least you like her by the way you refer to her."

"Oh, I love children. The circumstances of their birth are not their fault. It is their parents who are to blame for making some of them stepchildren."

"You are punching me below the belt. It hurts."

"Don't you think it hurts when the man you are going steady with turns out to have already started a family?"

66

"I have not started a family. I only have this little girl without mother care. Yes, I want to get married to somebody who will love me enough to accept my situation, and with whom I can start a family, the third member of which will be Mabel."

"I think I better be going. I have some work to do for tomorrow."

"That is fine, I'll escort you home. But let me apologise for the way your visit turned out this morning. You were hurting and did not enjoy it."

Jack decided not to contact Monica for a few days to allow her to get used to the idea of Mabel. It was very difficult not to ring her or meet her to reassure her of his commitment to her. But he persevered for three days. The fourth day he rang her early in the morning before she went to teach. "Monica, I miss you so much. What are your classes like today?"

"I have classes until midday."

"Can we have lunch somewhere?"

"That would be nice. I have missed you, too."

Jack was happy. He picked up Monica from the school at one o'clock and they had lunch together. After lunch, they sat under a tree and filled each other in on events of the last few days. Thereafter, their relationship grew even stronger than before. They met everyday and frequently visited each other's home. Monica and Mabel became great friends and the little girl sometimes accompanied her father on his visits to Monica's home.

Three months later, Jack said, "Monica, Saturday is Mabel's birthday. I want to take her and her friends to Didi's Amusement Park. I don't think I shall manage them alone. Will you come and help me?"

The request and the realisation that he needed her touched her. "Yes, of course, Jack. It will be a pleasure."

That Saturday, Jack picked up Monica in his father's car at ten in the morning. On reaching Makindye, they found Mabel and her friends ready and eagerly waiting. "Daddy, daddy, can we go now?"

"We will be going soon. But how about greeting Aunt Monica first!"

Mabel wrapped her tiny arms around Monica's legs and Monica scooped her up and hugged and kissed her.

"Happy birthday, Mabel!" And from her handbag, she produced a colourfully wrapped present.

Mabel sat down and unwrapped the present, and found a cute teddy bear. She was overjoyed.

"Daddy, daddy, look at my teddy bear!"

67

"Oh, it is lovely, Mabel! So what do you say to Aunt Monica?"

"Thank you, Aunt Monica," she said as she hugged both her teddy bear and Monica at the same time. Monica's heart went out to the little girl.

Monica was hugging the other children when Jack's mother called out, "All right, kids, come and have some juice before you go."

"Good morning, Mama. I have been imprisoned by the children, I have not greeted you," she said with a hint of laughter in her voice.

"Good morning, Monica. That is as it should be. The children seem to adore you."

After the juice and plenty of cakes and biscuits, Jack drove them to Didi's Amusement Park. The children were in the back seat, and Monica in front, beside him. Something stirred in him and he resolved to keep Monica by his side the rest of his life.

At Didi's Amusement Park, while the children were having fun, Jack and Monica watched over them. "Let us sit under that shed. We can still see the children from there."

Under the shed, Jack turned to Monica, "Monica, I cannot go on like this. I want to be with you all the time. I want you to be my wife. Will you marry me?" He was looking into her eyes to see if there was still doubt there. There was no doubt in the eyes swimming in tears. Monica looked back at him to see if there was sincerity in his. She saw not only sincerity but tenderness in his eyes.

"Yes, Jack, I shall be honoured to marry you."

They were in a public place so Jack could only hug Monica and give her a peck on her cheek. But the gesture conveyed so much to her.

"And Jack, when we are married, I shall not want to hear the word STEPDAUGHTER in our home because I hate it. Mabel shall be our daughter, and she shall be a sister to the other children who may come. NOT a stepsister."

"I think you are an angel sent to sort me out." He gave her another hug and another tiny kiss.

The Leopardess

Rose Rwakasisi

"Ted, Ted dear," Anna called from the children's bedroom.

"Yes, madam," Ted responded. As usual, he was not sure of what to expect from his sister-in-law. Sometimes she was welcoming and at other times, hostile to him. Anna suddenly appeared in the sitting room, vigorously wiping her delicate hands with a hand towel.

"Ted, you are a man now, even if not a better man than your brother George," Anna started with a funny smile.

"Eh, well," Ted responded, cautiously.

"What do you think about Jane - speaking as a man, of course? Is she really beautiful?" Anna inquired seriously.

"Well…" Ted said again, with a tentative smile. "Well-uh-uh-mmm, as it is often said, 'Beauty lies in the eyes of the beholder'."

"Surely what does your brother see in her?" Anna asked. "Though she looks younger than her age, everybody knows the woman is beyond four decades! If he had fallen for a young girl, I would have been ready to face the competition. I would have understood; but this old woman, men can be so blind!"

"Madam, have you forgotten the old saying that what attracts a man to an ugly woman is always hidden from the beautiful one, like you," Ted said, his eyes critically studying her. Anna was embarrassed by the message in his eyes. She decided to go to her bedroom and later came back with a ruffled photograph of Jane in a swimsuit.

"Look at her photograph, perhaps you can judge better when looking at her," Anna said as she put Jane's ruffled photograph on the table and continued to iron it with the back of her left hand. "Look at her! See the wide chimneys called a nose, those wide flat lips and the short forehead! And tell me, where does the beauty reside?"

There was a long silence as they both studied the photograph, one critically and the other with amusement. Ted almost blurted out something but he stopped himself in time. When he stole a glance at Anna's face, he saw a huge tear about to drop. He remembered the many parcels and letters he had carried from George to Jane's executive flat and he was filled with remorse. But he was also very pleased to see Jane shedding tears. He could clearly remember how he used to cry of hunger when he was in primary seven. If his classes went beyond six, he would run to her flat only to find the house-girl cleaning the supper dishes. There would be no supper left for him. That was the trying time when George had left him to keep an eye on his young wife while he was doing *kyeyo* in Japan. Whoever knew that one day, I, Ted would be a respectable man and Anna would get her punishment, he thought.

Suddenly, Ted looked up. Anna blinked back her eyes. She looked scared, and very unhappy. She looked desperately at Ted for a solution. "I fear old George thinks heaven of her," Anna confided in Ted.

"But how can he?" Ted said with exaggerated concern in his voice. "Perhaps he is deceiving you to make you jealous. How about that?"

She smiled as she licked some tears from her upper lip. "I hope so," she said. "I really hope so."

"Don't you trust George anymore?" Ted asked.

"Sometimes I do, but sometimes he does things that make me feel foolish. For example, there is tomorrow's wedding at Namirembe Cathedral. He is the best man and also responsible for the invitations. Only wedded couples were invited, I was told."

"Fortunately, I am not married. And between you, sis and me, I am planning to remain a bachelor for the next one hundred years," Ted interrupted her.

"But you must come. George is the best man and he asked me to go with you. But remember to leave when the party is about to end. I must return with George. Though only wedded couples are invited, I will not be surprised to see that leopardess, Jane march in. She never misses big parties! That woman!" Anna said, as she struck the table with her clenched delicate fist. When she looked around, the table was decorated with rivulets of soda from Ted's glass.

***

The church service was superb. The Archbishop himself officiated at the ceremony. All the big names in town were present. Ted almost did not mind the ordeal of standing beside the woman he abhorred, at the cocktail. If she was the price he had to pay to rub shoulders with the cream of society, perhaps it was worthwhile, he thought.

They were all merry, laughing heartily till the 'leopardess' walked in. Her face lacked the classic beauty, but her enchanting smile was worth millions of shillings. She had a terrific figure and wherever she passed,

70

men gaped and women cursed. For this occasion, she was dressed in a short-sleeved, simple tailored cream- dress. No necklace, no decorations; just a simple dress was all she needed to steal the show. Like a house snake, she glided silently to the side of her late brother's widow, who was standing near the entrance unaccompanied. "Enjoying yourself, sister?" Jane asked.

"Oh, yes thank you."

With a mischievous smile all over her face, Jane said to her, "I know I am not wanted here by everybody present, but, since I am here, I will try to make the best of the occasion."

"But I want you here. As a matter of fact, thanks for coming. I was feeling terribly out of place," Mary said warmly.

"No, not even you. I embarrass you among your moral friends."

"Stop that, Jane. You know I lost all my friends when I lost him. It's only you I can count on now," Mary said sincerely.

"Now, listen to me, old pussycat," Jane said to her, "I came here uninvited." When she got no response, she asked, "Are you listening to me?"

Like one awakened from a long dream, Mary jerked back. Then she confessed to Jane, "No. I was listening to the mother of the bride. I was imagining what it will be like when my time for speeches comes. It is mainly during ceremonies like this that I miss your brother most." She looked up as tears gathered in her eyes.

"Stop that and remember always 'to cross the river when you reach it', as he used to say to us," Jane admonished her.

"Yes, yes," Mary agreed. A teardrop escaped. She wiped it with the back of her hand.

"Now listen to me, sis, and stop being a sissy," Jane went on. "I came uninvited, but I came because a woman rang me and provoked me. I have come to show her and hers how bitchy I can be when someone dares to cross me."

"Jane, don't use such language," Mary begged. "Somebody might hear you. Don't give people reason to say more bad things about you. You know how much it hurts me when I hear so much rubbish fabricated about you." Jane gave her a sweet smile and walked away to mix with the crowd. Mary mused about how Jane could be so sweet to her and spiteful to others.

Jane was like a magnet. All eyes turned to her. From somewhere, a short, lean, tough-looking little man accosted her with a glass of wine. She brushed the glass away with her hand as if by accident and it fell, splashing wine onto the nearby guests. As if to save the man from any further embarrassment, Jane took his half-full tumbler of beer and gulped it. Then she walked on. Very soon she was the centre of attraction. Even the eyes of the bridegroom were riveted to her. The wedding ceremony had turned sour.

Then she beckoned to the manager of the Fathers' Union Bank with her left middle finger. The fat bank manager with an extended stomach zig-zagged his way through the crowds to her side in record time.

"Take me out of this place. Take me out before I cause a scene," Jane commanded him. The two disappeared. All the women sighed with relief to see her back. The wife of the bank manager disappeared to the ladies' room to adjust her make-up. The lucky ladies shared her grief silently. All the men felt cheated and lost their mood for the party.

"Ladies and gentlemen, the bride and bridegroom are going to cut the cake. You are all requested to stand up and clap for them," the Master of Ceremonies announced.

Everybody stood up, clapped and laughed in relief. Another announcement soon followed, "The Best Man, Dr. George is wanted outside in connection with a patient he operated on yesterday. He is requested to go outside for a few minutes of consultation." George went out but whom did he find waiting for him near his car!

"George, don't panic. I am the patient. I need a prescription," Jane said, looking very serious.

"You bitch," George hissed under his breath. "But Jane, I am the Best Man, how could you interrupt the party like this!"

"How could I have known you were busy? You did not invite me."

"But Jane ..." he pleaded.

"Because I am not wedded, so I have to be locked out of society?"

"No, but be fair, at least this once."

"Make your choice today! What time do you pick me up?" she asked him as she eyed him like a leopard about to spring upon its prey.

"But, Jane, stop being unfair. You very well know that I am a married man. I have duties to perform in that respect. One of them is driving my wife home after the After Party," George said firmly.

"Tonight of all nights, she will go home alone like I always do," Jane retorted. Then she added, "At midnight, I will be waiting for you near the Post Office." Then she marched away, swinging her behind with exaggeration.

"Okay, see you then," George addressed her back. He walked away feeling as if a bucket of ice-cold water had been poured over him.

As soon as she reached her car, Jane rang another guest at the same wedding party. This one had no qualms about leaving his wife stranded. "Meet you at eleven p.m," he agreed. They spent the rest of the weekend together at Collins Hotel.

Before the party ended, George explained to his wife that he had a patient in a serious condition to attend to at the hospital. Feeling victorious, she kissed him goodnight and walked to a special-hire taxi which dropped her at their posh Kololo residence.

When George looked in the parking lot at midnight, Jane's car was not there. He instead found a note on the side mirror of his car telling him that she had changed her mind about meeting him.

"That bitch!" he cursed. He put the key into the lock and opened the door. He then lingered out for a while wondering where to go.

When he woke up twelve hours later, he was in a hospital bed. He was told that the force of the explosion had thrown him a safe distance away from his car. Who had planted the bomb under his car, the police wondered. George was scared when he was told how he had narrowly escaped death. He dared not speak out his thoughts.

She sent a bouquet of flowers and a card to him at the hospital. The card read, "The leopard skin you wanted is too expensive for you. Somebody else has bid higher. I believe the god she prays to answers her prayers. Lucky her. Bye and wishing you a quick recovery."

Vengeance Of The Gods

Beatrice Lamwaka

"Now that she is dead, I must deal with her spirit so that my children and I will not be affected by that butter-wouldn't-melt-in-thy-mouth witch," muttered Lalobo as she looked around to make sure nobody was watching. She had to slide the feather from the middle of her thighs in such a way that no one would guess what she was doing.

She slouched towards the newly cemented grave of her co-wife, *Min* Okello (mother of Okello). "She thought she deserved everything, and I, like a dog, was to just watch," she said loudly to herself, scratching her kinky hair. "I have children, too, but they have deserted me." She sniffed and added with a sneer, "Her children buried her like a princess, a lavish funeral. Let's see who wins, if not I, mother of them all."

She glanced at Otto, who was too drunk to even tell his hands from his legs, let alone realise that he had defecated on himself. Lalobo turned away in disgust and hissed, "I had to destroy him: he spoke too much. I am not sorry about it." She let out an ear-piercing demonic laugh and added, "He ate it in his food, that bull! I, Lalobo waste no time on people who stand in my way."

Not bothered by a soul, Lalobo parted her legs to remove the Malibu stork feather. The medicine woman had instructed her to keep it in between her thighs till the afternoon of the eve of *Min* Okello's last funeral rites. She pulled it out easily, since she wore no knickers, and buried it in the mound of soil next to where the deceased's head was supposed to be facing. Just like the medicine woman, Acen had instructed her.

Min Okello had died of the swelling of the stomach, coupled with a strange ailment called *two rec* believed to have come from Sudan. This disease normally left its victim with a scaly skin and a mouth producing rotten substance resembling dead maggots. Her children, who lived in the capital city, Kampala, took her to all the hospitals there but the doctors could not diagnose her disease. Even Doctor Smith Clarke, the white specialist in strange African diseases, shook his head in defeat and referred them to the local medicine men. They at last found a medicine man who seemed to know the disease and how to treat it. But Lalobo's intrusion and supervision made him leave an irritated man. Efforts to bring him back were futile.

Lalobo flattened the earth carefully to hide the feather, which was to put *Min* Okello' spirit at rest. This was to stop her from taking revenge from the other world. Contented that the last ritual was complete, Lalobo decided to visit Acen on her way to the spring. Lalobo had no friend in the village; Acen was the only person she could confide in. Most women hated her. It was rumoured in the village that she had got her husband, Latim, through witchcraft.

Acen was a frail looking woman in her thirties. Her ears were enormous like a rabbit's. She had given birth to four boys who had all died at barely the age of one. What perturbed people was that her husband did not chase her away, neither did he hurl insults or derogatory remarks at her. He instead resorted to getting more wives. Poor Acen could not complain, for she had no children of her own.

Acen was now seated under a tree. As Lalobo approached, she could see that Acen had just shaven the sides of her head, leaving just enough hair for two rows that stood majestically in the middle of her small head. This was a new hairstyle, for sure.

"What do you want now from me, you wretched woman? Haven't you killed enough people already?" Acen asked Lalobo jokingly, as she walked towards her.

"Enough is never enough," Lalobo said and laughed.

"Then you have come for more killer charms, eeeeeh?" Acen asked.

"Nooooooo," replied Lalobo. "I have come to share my happiness with you. Don't you know what our people say, that one hand does not open the vagina? Ha ha ha," they both laughed like young girls.

"You woman and your dirty mind," Acen said. "Is that the best saying you could have used?"

"I am not the composer of proverbs," Lalobo said.

"I see. So if you want me to share your happiness, where is the cock?"

"Next time," Lalobo answered, looking at the mat. Acen got the signal and like a good mannered child, she moved away a bit to allow Lalobo room to sit. A worried look appeared on Lalobo's face. "Are you sure that I am a free woman? Without vengeance to worry about?" she asked.

"Have I ever promised you air, tell me, have I?" retorted Acen.

"You know I killed *Min* Okello out of jealousy. She was a good woman. Even if she had sons and I, on the other hand, was cursed with girls whose bastards fill my house, that was still no reason to kill her, you know," Lalobo said, worried. "My worry, my friend Acen, is that the gods may turn against me."

"You see, that is what I was worried about. Why? Why?"

"Why what? " Lalobo asked, opening her palms.

"You have reported yourself to the gods. When you commit a crime like you have, you never say it aloud because the gods are always listening. Now they know you are a killer."

"Oh god Lagooro of my forefathers, what am I going to do?"

"Don't worry, my dear friend, we can also deal with the gods. But this time you have to bleed money, because we need a virgin bull, a white goat, water from the middle of the lake, a root of the *kituba* tree, a..."

"Please do not continue," Lalobo interrupted. "Where in the world do you expect me to find a virgin bull and all that? You will soon tell me to bring a fresh head."

"You must finish what you began. Water does not flow backwards."

"You said the feather would be the last. Now where are all these virgin bulls, white goats, tree roots and whatever else going to come from?"

"Woman, you never finish with these things."

" But..."

"No buts; just do as I say."

" I cannot afford it."

" It is not about what you can afford. Just do as I say in two days. You never know what these scorned gods are capable of doing."

" I came here to celebrate, not..."

"Celebrate after killing an innocent woman! What do you expect after you and your big mouth couldn't keep quiet about your deeds."

" I am confused, are you against me?"

" It is not about taking sides. It is about what you have done. You killed an innocent woman and I helped...oh no! I didn't say it. Listen carefully, Lalobo, do as I have told you and within two days. Excreta is dealt with while it is still fresh."

"Fine. I thought you were supposed to side with mortals, not spirits. But I was wrong, very wrong."

"Just do as told."

"Let me leave your sight before you add a yellow sheep, a blue hen or a wingless eagle to the list." She stalked away angrily and left wondering where on earth she would find all those things.

Lalobo was now faced with a dilemma and needed to be alone. She knew that back home, guests for *Min* Okello's last funeral rites must have begun arriving. She tried to hurry to the spring to get the water she should have got hours ago but her legs felt as if heavy logs were tied around them.

At home, the relatives had started arriving. *Min* Okello's children came in cars with loads of things as if it was a party, Lalobo thought resentfully. She glanced at her stepdaughter Adong, who was a replica of her mother *Min* Okello. Adongo ran towards her stepmother and hugged her passionately. She loved her very much, though Lalobo treated her coolly, making her feel like a child caught licking sugar. But that did not bother Adong in the least: Lalobo would always be her mother.

"Mother, I am happy to see you! How are you?"   Adong greeted Lalobo.

"I am fine. You no longer come to see us," Lalobo complained.

"I have been busy, mother."

"Don't worry, my daughter, we will survive."

"I will come and see you again, I promise."

"My daughter, I have a big problem. I don't have any money. I tried to brew local beer but it was too dilute and nobody bought even a tot. I need money desperately."

"Don't worry, mother, we will arrange everything."

"No, I need something for the pocket."

"Don't worry. Everything is under control."

Seeing that her daughter was determined not to give her money, Lalobo walked away. She had to get another prey, but wherever she went, everyone turned her down. This sent the villagers talking. Lalobo was the kind of person who would not even beg for salt from the neighbours. "Perhaps something is amiss," they conjectured. One woman even said, "Lalobo is not herself these days." Sometimes she made a mistake and asked the same person twice for money, giving a different reason each time.

That night, Lalobo was awakened by a terrible dream. She dreamt that she was being bitten by babies who said the gods had sent them as their agents and told her the worst was yet to come. Lalobo quickly got out of bed. She had to get money this time by all means.

"Morning, mother," Adong greeted her.

Bad omen, Lalobo said to herself silently. Then loudly, "Morning." Why does she have to look like her dead mother!

Lalobo walked towards the villagers who were flocking in. Most of them came for the food and the local brew, *arege*. The young girls were doing most of the work. Bored, Lalobo had nothing to do but greet the villagers and watch what was going on. The compound was extremely busy. People were fetching water, bringing firewood, others bringing all sorts of food.

The elders were seated outside on low stools. They drank beer from gourds and spoke in low voices as they waited for the medicine man, Chan, who would fetch the spirit of *Min* Okello from the unknown place to be questioned about her welfare.

Chan arrived late in the afternoon with a group of assistants, all dressed in brown cow skins and *bomo*, a creeping plant. He wore a hat made of feathers and adorned with beads, cowry shells, claws of birds and snake skins. He held a skull in his hands. On reaching *Min* Okello's hut, he trembled like an aspen in the wind. This was an indication that her sprit was disturbed.

Lalobo was frightened but remembering what the measures she had taken against such an eventuality, she felt calm again. In her mind, she even had hatched a plan to distract Chan if anything went wrong. Inside the hut, a stool was given to Chan to sit on, while the assistants rattled the gourds to the family members and the elders who had joined them. Then Chan began a familiar song to which everybody chorused a response as they clapped their hands. Chan danced, throwing his legs here and there, rapping, cursing, appealing to the unknown. Suddenly, Chan began speaking in *Min* Okello's voice.

"I am chained, set my spirit free." *Min* Okello's voice spoke.

"By who?" the elders asked,

"She," the voice spoke again.

"Who?"

"Lalobo, my co-wife."

Chan trembled, sent a cataloguing gaze around while everyone stared at Lalobo. She sniffed, got up but was shoved down by the assistants. Chan got up, walking in the same springy way like *Min* Okello used to, prancing from one corner to the other. Lalobo, scared that Chan, now possessed by *Min* Okello, was aiming at her, fled from the hut. People got out and scrambled after her, leaving Chan and his assistants.

"She killed *Min* Okello. Get her!" somebody screamed. Everybody ran after Lalobo, hitting her with stones, saucepans and potatoes as she ran. Cries of children and shouts of elders could be heard from every corner. Complete anarchy had taken over.

Lalobo fell down heavily but people were still coming after her. They had cassava sticks in their hands they had uprooted from a nearby garden. Some strong men carried big stones all of which came crashing down upon her body.

"Spare me! Spare me! Let me explain," Lalobo cried out.

But nobody could hear her now. They were all thirsty for blood and blood was what they would settle for. "Kill the sorceress, kill the sorceress," they chanted. Children, too, joined in the stoning and chanting as if it was a game of dodge the ball. Soon, the stoning and chanting died down. What was left of Lalobo was a horrifying sight of blood, weapons and flesh mixed in one messy heap. Everybody turned away. Nobody said a word. Their faces reflected the horror of what was left of Lalobo.

End Of A Journey

Waltraud Ndagijimana

Everything was still at rest when the faint morning light turned grey over the distant bare Ntungamo hills. Only here and there an early bird stirred and a hesitant chirping could be heard. It would not be long before the first rays of the sun pushed away the darkness that had lain over the land, covering all its misery and poverty like a heavy dark blanket. The land lay still, silent and enduring. It waited for the end of fear and torment, torture and death.

The woman pulled the threadbare blanket up to her thin shoulders for more warmth. She was shivering again. "I must get up," she said loudly. Her weakened body felt every mound of the mud floor through the thin mattress. Slowly, wearily, she turned herself, mindful not to disturb the little boy sleeping peacefully beside her. The boy moved just a little, turning his head on the flat pillow, his curly dark hair dump from sleep. Today he would not go to school — today they would leave home.

She looked around the small house. It was not much of a home, anyway, only a shaky table and two rough chairs. Her mattress was placed behind an old curtain in a corner next to the Blue Band carton where she kept her clothes. Yet these four walls had given her shelter and a little comfort for many years. Through the cracks in the shutter of the small window, she had watched the heavy army trucks of the different regimes roar past on the road below. Here, she had barricaded herself behind the door, when a gang of uniformed men had approached her house. Maybe they had been put off by her all too humble hut, only to kill her neighbour and his wife, leaving the children screaming in horror at the sight of the mutilated bodies of their parents. The woman's fingers tensed and the hollow feeling in her stomach returned whenever she remembered the scene of desolation. Insecurity was all round them, death had become a major part of their life.

At the final rooster call, she slowly turned the key in the door, picked up her bundle of clothes and took her son's hand. She breathed heavily. She had little strength left in her and every little movement seemed to cost her so much effort, so much will and energy. The boy hopped along the narrow path, his bare feet hardly touching the ground and paying lit-tle attention to his mother. The grass was still wet from the morning dew and it left small cool droplets on the boy's legs. He seemed to have no worry in the world as he rushed in excited anticipation towards the asphalt road. When he stopped suddenly, he heard his mother's laboured breath and saw her coming unsteadily down the hill. Her eyes looked bright and seemed to have lost the dullness of the previous months. Sometimes he could not understand her painful twists and little moans that seemed to have taken her over completely. She did not smile so often any more. He jumped down the last metres of the path and sat by the roadside, his foot drawing irregular circles in the sand.

"Where are we going? I am hungry," he said in a matter of-fact-voice that was not going to betray the excitement he felt. He had never been anywhere far from home.

"I shall buy you some cakes on the way," the woman said, ignoring the first question. The boy seemed satisfied with the answer, the prospect of some succulent cakes making him hum a tune. Behind him, his mother sat down heavily on a mound of earth. She had tied a colourful scarf around her head. Her eyes seemed too large in her thin drawn face. She was looking at her hands, then rubbing the palms together as if to give them some comforting warmth.

From the distance, the boy heard the rumbling of the bus. As he jumped up excitedly, he saw it crawling up the hill like a huge caterpillar. First he only caught a glimpse of mattresses and other odd pieces of furniture tied onto its top, and swaying precariously as it rounded a bend. The noise increased as the old vehicle drew nearer. With screeching brakes and a loud puff, it stopped right next to its prospective passengers.

"Kabale - Kisoro" said the small wooden board behind the screen. The boy looked at his mother who hesitantly picked up her bundle, then halt-ed a moment, drew in a sharp breath and gazed at the soft green hills around them. She seemed to be memorising this picture of early morning peace and tranquillity. Her eyes blinked as the top of her hand briskly rubbed over them as if to erase what she had seen. Then she straightened her back and followed her son who was already waving and calling ani-matedly inside. The conductor looked at her and asked where she was going. The woman mumbled her destination and slowly placed the fare in his outstretched hand and secured her ticket.

The bus started with a jerk and wound its way along the mountains, climbing each approaching hill with more and more effort. The windows were mud-spluttered and the boy could hardly see anything outside. His eyes wandered around the bus, inspecting the passengers who seemed drowsy and exhausted. Some youths on the seat behind him were making crude jokes, repeatedly bursting into laughter. The boy strained his ears but he only caught the odd word in a language that was strange to him.

After what seemed only a short time, the bus stopped at the roadside. Fruit and cake sellers swarmed around noisily, advertising their goods. One of them came right up to the woman and she bought the cakes the boy had been longing for. He closed his eyes when his teeth bit into the soft texture. This was a rare treat and he made small bites, letting them linger in his mouth, enjoying the sweetness. He counted the remaining cakes in the polythene bag, which he held tightly — only four! These he would eat later, the journey was still long, his mother had said.

As the bus pulled out of the little trading centre, the murram road became hard and bumpy. Innumerable potholes were filled with muddy water and every time the bus sank its tyres into one of them, it sent splutters up to the windows. Thousands of water drops formed small rivulets, which made their way to the ground again. The boy looked at their dancing and dazzling performance fascinated. But eventually, his eyes grew heavy and he fell asleep, his head lolling between the fringe of the cushioned chair and the window glass. The voices of the other passengers grew faint and distant, and their laughter to no more than a giggle. The woman dozed off, too, her head leaning towards her son.

Suddenly, the bus came to an abrupt stop. Lake Bunyonyi lay still and unruffled but from outside came the noise of agitated angry voices. Something hard hit the door and the passengers were suddenly roused from their sleep and looked up apprehensively. The boy's eyes searched for his mother's, who at that time was seized by a violent bout of coughing. Her eyes widened in terror as she fought to regain her breath. Her chest heaved, expanded, collapsed again only to be seized by a greater panic. In her agony, she pulled the scarf from her head and held it to her mouth, but not quickly enough. Her son gazed in terror at the bright red spot that coloured the scarf. As she slowly pulled in the life-giving air, tears of exhaustion streamed down her face. But she wiped them away fearfully, at the same time trying to give the boy next to her some confidence. She was only betrayed by the anguish in her eyes.

The other passengers had tried to divide their attention between the angry voice outside and the woman fighting for breath. Now they anxiously turned their heads towards the door again, which was roughly thrown open. The muzzle of a gun appeared first, slowly and menacingly. Then, as if he feared something from the passengers inside, a tall figure in a ragged uniform slowly came into view. The woman's heart stopped a bit as she gazed at the figure. Her son's hand instinctively found hers and she gripped it and held it tight.

"*Toka wote!*" the figure ordered. At the sound of the harsh tone, a small child started wailing. The brutal face turned into the direction of the small voice. Terrified by the hostile stare, the child's mother quickly pulled her breast from under her blouse and pushed the nipple into the eager mouth. As if waiting for appraisal, the mother looked at the man but he avoided her eyes, pulling his mouth into a small black line. He did not say another word but he lifted his heavy gun and gestured to the passengers to stand up and leave the bus. Slowly, the men and women stood up from their seats, hampered by the luggage heaped on their laps. The odour of sweaty bodies filled the stale air.

As the passengers left the bus, their bags and bundles were seized from them, some thrown violently back into the bus, narrowly missing bodies that were pushing forwards. The woman and her son slowly climbed down from the bus. She saw a group of not less than twenty uniformed men sitting under a cluster of trees. These were watching, with sadistic amusement, the passengers being herded from the bus warily take their position as far from them as possible.

"Separate the women, let us look at them," a cruel voice shouted. Seized by sheer terror, the women clung tightly together as they were separated from the men. A huge man, his uniform in tatters, looked at his kingdom of cruelty and fear. He lay his hand on the shoulders of a young girl and pulled her violently from the elderly woman she was clinging to. As the muzzle of the gun was pushed hard into her back, she lost her balance and let go. With an iron grip, the tall man dragged her behind in the shadow of a dilapidated unipot, grinning at his comrades as they cheered him.

The small group of women drew more closely together as two more uniformed men approached them. The woman felt a tight grip on her arm and knew that her fate was sealed, but she would not give in to this overpowering villain without a fight. Her son had also clutched her in total panic. "No!" she screamed. "I am not well and I am with my child, please...my son ...here...you see." She stumbled in the muddy water and the brown liquid shot up and splashed her to her ankles as she pulled the bloody scarf from her pocket. "I shall make you sick…" As if she had waved a magic stick, the soldier pushed her roughly aside. She fell down, one hand still clutching her son's, the other holding the bloody scarf. The man looked at her in contempt and made his way back to the group of women.

"What did the man want with you?" her son asked fearfully, his voice trembling. As he watched, another woman, much younger in age, was hauled from the group and pushed roughly behind the hut. "We are lucky we didn't have to go behind the hut," he now said, quite pleased with himself.

From behind the hut, the woman could hear some subdued sobs of the young girl, then some angry voice and a slap. While the boy strained his ears to make out what was going on in that secret place, his mother made an effort to involve him in some conversation. After some time, he grew tired and started looking around the place.

One of the women, not young any more, came from behind the dark shadows holding the young girl. She had put an arm around her, speaking softly. Two more women reappeared, one looking defiant, the other looking at the group of male passengers who seemed to be gazing in a void, their feet rooted to the ground. Others gave their shoestrings an aura of importance. Neither group spoke. A force that could not be argued with had taken possession of them. The only thing they could do now was wait.

Some of the uniformed rogues had entered the bus. From outside, one could hear boxes being broken, locks discarded. Whole bundles of clothes were flung through the windows. The woman saw her bundle thrown close to her feet. She was about to go for it when a strong hand of another woman held her back. "Don't push your luck. You have escaped once, let those things go."

Time seemed to stand still. Minutes dragged into hours and the people sat there like waste being washed ashore by a violent river. Anything could happen to them any time.

Finally, under a lot of cruel laughter, the loot was carried away and the air of oppression became lighter when, in a coarse voice, they were told to get back into the bus. Hastily, they scrambled up, pushing and shoving each other, trying to escape from the place of inhumanity and terror. None of them bothered about their property any more: everything of value had been taken, anyway. But the boy divided under his seat and tri- umphantly reappeared holding the polythene bag with his four cakes, some reduced to crumbs. His mother smiled and patted his head.

As the bus slowly and hesitantly drove off, a bullet passed above it, narrowly missing it. Derisive laughter followed as the driver accelerated. The ordeal was over but what lay ahead of them?

Outside, the evening came up slowly. The green hills receded in the mist, the clouds lay low and a cold wind came up from the lake. It was going to rain and they still had another two hours to go.

The woman felt exhausted and could hardly breath. The anguish of the afternoon had taken its toll. Her chest was tight, her breathing very painful and her head thumped. The other passengers sat in silence, each trying to come to grips with what had happened, in their own way.

As the bus lumbered on, night took over the world. The rain fell slowly and the trees were now mere silhouettes in the deepening darkness. Gradually, the rough road descended towards the valley and somewhere near a mud track, the woman made out the Mutolere Hospital signpost.

"I have had enough problems for one day," the driver shouted through the bus. "Diesel is little and if we pass through the hospital, we might get stuck there before we reach Kisoro town. You must find your own way there now." The woman froze. She did not know anybody in the town.

"No," she said to herself, "he can't do this to me." But there was no pleading with the man. He stopped some good distance from the town near a beaten track. "Follow this path: it is just a few kilometres from your hospital," he said.

As the woman and her son stepped out into the night, they held on to each other. It was a very dark night and a sense of total loss overcame them. The rain had changed into a steady drizzle and a cold wind made them shiver. The woman pulled her son closer. Her teeth were chattering and an ice-cold grip held her throat. She tightened her grip on the boy, trying to give him the reassurance she herself needed so badly.

Slowly, they stumbled on in the darkness, hitting their feet on the sharp lava stones. There was no sign of life anywhere. They had no idea where they were and whether the direction they were taking was the right one.

There was not a soul near the roadside. All the little village bars that had in former days bristled with life and resounded with happy laughter of men, had long closed now. These were times when one did not move about at night. Too much had happened lately.

Suddenly, the woman was shaken by another violent burst of coughing. She stopped walking and pressed her hands to her chest. As the bout shook her violently, she slowly slid on a grassy patch. The hot sticky liq-

85

uid filled her mouth again and she spat it out. She spat again and again until her breathing became shallow and she lay exhausted. The boy had started crying silently.

"Don't cry," she whispered. "Just give me a little time." He crouched near her and they sat holding each other. The rain had stopped but it was very cold. The woman knew she had to make an effort to stand up but she felt terribly weak. Her cheeks were burning and she felt an urge to just sit there and let things happen to her. The boy seemed to have fallen asleep next to her. So she sat and waited for a little while longer until she regained enough strength to continue. "Let's go," she shook him awake and he hastily stood up and felt for her hand. Together, they stumbled on in the darkness for what was just a few minutes but seemed like eternity to them.

They passed trees, their branches hitting their faces and thorns scratching their legs. The woman could hardly walk but she had to continue for her son's sake. Every part of her body was now aching, every breath a torment. She sat down again and again as the minutes of the dark night slowly ticked away. They had come nowhere near the hospital; they did not even know if they were moving in circles.

Suddenly, the boy saw a small flickering light in the distance. A ray of hope for them in this desolate night. The woman seemed to regain her energy but as they came nearer to the house, she again fell down heavily. "Go to the house and tell the people inside that we need help. Tell them that we need shelter and that we are looking for the way to the hospital…"

"Mother, I am scared. I don't know those people."

"Just go. You have to be a big boy now."

"Okay," the boy breathed, swallowing hard.

Slowly, he moved towards the house, repeatedly turning to glance back into the darkness. After only a few paces, he had lost sight of his mother lying there and he started to sob as he moved forward. He felt his way forward, guided by the flickering light until he was standing before the door. As soon as his hesitant knock was heard inside, all voices fell silent and the little gleam of light was extinguished. After a lot of whispering, somebody cleared his voice and asked, "Who is that?"

"It's me. I have come for help."

"Go away. We cannot help you." This time the voice was very loud, drumming in the boy's ears.

"Please help me. My mother is sick outside. We need someone to help us," he pleaded.

"You need to go to the hospital. Isn't that the story you told our neighbours two nights ago, and when they opened the door the soldiers came from behind the bushes and rushed in the house? You go and see what is left of that house and the people there."

The boy did not understand what the man was talking about. But from the sound of his voice, he knew he would not get any help from here. He tried just one more time, pleading and crying but there was only stony silence inside.

Slowly, he turned away, stumbling back into darkness, crying out softly for his mother. He heard her voice that was now barely audible. When he finally came close to her, he just sat by her side. She did not even ask what had happened at the house. She slowly pulled him towards her, pulled her sweater over him and the two lay motionless side by side. It was not until next morning that two early risers from the village found a young boy sleeping peacefully next to his dead mother.

ARAC Monica de Nyeko comes from Kitgum district. She studied at Gulu High School and Katikamu SDA School respectively. She is currently studying for a Bachelor of Arts degree with Education at Makerere University. She is a member of FEMRITE and is working on her first novel, *Spears of Fate*. Her poem, *Damn You,* has been published in *Berlin Poetry Anthology 2001*. It was one of the poems read at the German Literature Festival held in Berlin June 2001.

***

BARYA Kiconco Mildred, holds a Bachelor of Arts degree in Literature from Makerere University. She studied at Kigezi High School. She writes short stories, plays, poems, magazine articles but has as yet to tackle a novel. Some of her poems have appeared in various journals in Uganda and USA. She is interested in the short-short story genre and most of her current short stories have been developed in this style. She is a regular contributor to *New Era* magazine and she runs the Resource Centre at FEMRITE.

***

BATANDA Jackee hails from Busia district. She attended Mary Hill High School and Bweranyangi Girls' Secondary School for her 'O' and 'A' Levels respectively. She went to the Institute of Teacher Education Kyambogo (ITEK) where she obtained a Diploma in Teacher Education in Art and Design.

Jackee is a member of FEMRITE and does some voluntary work. She writes for *The Sunday Monitor* newspaper and is a regular contributor to *New Era* Magazine, a publication of FEMRITE. She is currently working on a novel, *Epistle For Malaika* and a collection of short stories. She has a manuscript of poems not yet published

***

ETOORI Deborah was born in Tanzania but now lives in Uganda. She went to Tabora Girls' School and then joined Makerere College/University where she obtained a Diploma in Education, a Bachelor of Arts degree and a Master of Education degree. She taught English, Mathematics and Geography in various schools in Uganda before she joined Makerere University administration in 1966. She is now retired and spends most of her time writing mainly children's stories, two of which (*The Mlimbolimbo Tree* and *The Whale and His Family*) have been published by Fountain Publishers. Etoori also contributes articles to *New Era* Magazine.

***

KYOMUHENDO Goretti's first novel, *The First Daughter*, was published by Fountain Publishers, Kampala [1996] and became an instant success. Her second novel, *Secrets No More,* was published by FEMRITE Publications Limited [1999]. She has completed her third novel, *Whispers from Vera.* Kyomuhendo is the Co-ordinator of Uganda Women Writers' Association, FEMRITE, and an Honorary Fellow of Creative Writing of the University of Iowa, USA.

***

LAMWAKA Beatrice hails from Gulu district. She studied in Nsambya Girls Secondary School and Namugongo Senior Secondary School for 'O' and 'A' Levels respectively. She is currently studying for a Bachelor of Arts degree at Makerere University. She writes short stories, poems, and articles for the *New Era* magazine. She is currently working on her first novel. She is a member of FEMRITE.

***

MUNYARUGERERO Gashumba Winnie was born in Kisoro but grew up in Ruhinda, Bushenyi district. She went to Hormby Girls School, Gayaza High School and Makerere University where she graduated with a Bachelor of Arts honours degree in English and French. She has a Diploma in Education (equivalent) of the University of Besancon, France. Winnie writes for various magazines and newspapers. She is especially interested in the education of the girl child and issues concerning women and children.

***

NAMBOZO Beverley was born in 1976. She spent eight of her childhood years in England. She studied at Gayaza High School and Makerere College School for her 'O' and 'A' Levels respectively. She has a BA (Ed) with Literature in English and English Language as her teaching subjects from Makerere University. She is currently studying for a diploma in French at Alliance Francaise, Kampala. Beverley writes for *The Sunday Monitor* newspaper and has keen interest in gospel music and choreography. Presently, she is working on her first novel, *Edna's Tomorrow*, and an anthology of poetry and short stories . She has recently been appointed a teacher of History and English of secondary section at Rainbow International School.

***

NDAGIJIMANA Waltraud, was born July 9, 1949, in Neuss, Germany. She graduated in Education in 1972, at Aachen, Germany. She now lives in Mutolere, Bufumbira, Kisoro district and teaches Literature at St. Gertrude's Girls' Secondary School, Mutolere. Her short story, *The Key*, was broadcast on BBC World Service in 1996. She is presently working on a book of short stories.

***

OKOED Aimo Sandra comes from Soroti district and attended schools in Uganda, Kenya, the UK and USA. She holds a BA degree in Print Journalism with a minor in Sociology from Ithaca College, USA. She has always had an interest in creative writing but focuses mainly on feature writing. She is a regular contributor to *New Era* magazine, a publication of FEMRITE, and has written for the *Ithacan* and *Ithaca Times* (in the USA). One of her ambitions is to publish more of her short stories. She is currently working as a Senior Programme Officer at Akina Mama wa Afrika, Kampala.

***

RUTAGONYA Twongyeirwe Hilda was born in Kacherere, Kabale district. She attended Kacherere Primary School, Bishop Girls' School Muyebe, Uganda Martyrs High School Rubaga, National Teachers'College Nkozi and Makerere University where she graduated with an honours degree in Social Sciences. She is currently doing a Masters degree in Public Administration and Management at Makerere University. Her interests include creative writing and drama. Her short story, *Becoming A Woman*, was published in *A Woman's Voice*, an anthology of short stories published by FEMRITE. Some of her poems, too, have been published in magazines and journals. She is also a regular contributor to *New Era* magazine, a publication of FEMRITE.

***

RWAKASISI Rose, was born in Buhweju, Bushenyi district. She went to Kibubura Girls Primary School, Bweranyangi Girls Boarding School and Gayaza High School. She graduated with a B.Sc. and P.G.D Education from Makerere University. She has taught in many secondary schools in Uganda. Rwakasisi was basically trained by NCDC, Ministry of Education as a textbook writer. She writes for

children and two of her stories, *The Old Woman and the Shell* and *How Friends Became Enemies* were published by Fountain Publishers who are alson considering her other two stories, *How Goats Lost Their Tails* and *How Rats Escaped From The Trap*. Also in the pipeline is *The Broken Promise* due to be published by The Uganda Children's Writers and Illustrators Association. Rose also writes the Children's page in *New Era* Magazine.

***

TINDYEBWA Lillian was born in Rukungiri district, Southern Uganda. She holds a Bachelor of Arts degree of Makerere University. Her first novel, *Recipe for Disaster* was published by Fountain Pubilshers, Kampala [1994]. Her short story, *Looking For My Mother* was published in *A Woman's Voice*, an anthology of short stories published by FEMRITE Publications Limited [1998].

***

WANGUSA Ayeta Anne hails from Mbale district, Eastern Uganda. She went to Buganda Road Primary School, Mt. St. Mary's College Namagunga and Makerere High School. She holds a Bachelor of Arts honours degree and a Master of Arts degree in Literature of Makerere University. She is currently working as a sub-editor with Uganda's leading daily, *The New Vision*. Her first novel, *Memoirs of a Mother*, was published by FEMRITE Publications Limited [1998]. She is working on her second novel, *Restless Souls*. She is also an Honorary Fellow of Creative Writing of the University of Iowa, USA.

***

Wanja Josephine is a social economist. Born in Britain, she came to Uganda in 1961 and obtained Uganda citizenship in 1964. She has been married twice and is now widowed. She has seven children and four grandchildren.

She has published a number of professional articles but this is her first attempt at fiction.

***